M

W

REAR VIE

JAN 17

MAY

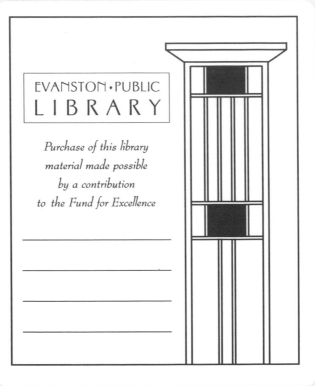

REAR VIEW

S T O R I E S

....

Pete Duval

A MARINER ORIGINAL

HOUGHTON MIFFLIN COMPANY

BOSTON · NEW YORK · 2004

For information about permission to reproduce selections
from this book, write to Permissions, Houghton Mifflin Company,
215 Park Avenue South, New York, New York 10003.

Visit our Web site: www.houghtonmifflinbooks.com.

Library of Congress Cataloging-in-Publication Data
Duval, Pete.
Rear view : stories / Pete Duval.
p.   cm.
"A Mariner original."
ISBN 0-618-44140-9
1. United States — Social life and customs — Fiction.
2. Blue collar workers — Fiction. 3. Working class — Fiction.
4. Catholics — Fiction. I. Title.
PS3604.U78R43 2004
813'.6 — dc22   2004047341

Book design by Melissa Lotfy

Printed in the United States of America

MP 10 9 8 7 6 5 4 3 2 1

Excerpt from "In Passing" from *Alive Together: New and Selected
Poems* by Lisel Mueller. Reprinted by permission of Louisiana State
University Press. Copyright © 1996 by Lisel Mueller.

Excerpt from "Tell Me Something Good," words and music by
Stevie Wonder. Copyright © 1974 (Renewed 2002) Jobete Music
Co., Inc., and Black Bull Music c/o EMI April Music, Inc. All rights
reserved. International copyright secured. Used by permission.

For Kim and for Nick

as if what exists, exists

so that it can be lost

and become precious

—LISEL MUELLER,
"In Passing"

ACKNOWLEDGMENTS

Some of these stories, in slightly different form, have appeared in the following publications: *Alaska Quarterly Review, Ascent, Chelsea, Exquisite Corpse, Grain, New Hampshire College Journal, Northwest Review, Oxford Magazine, West Branch.*

I would like to thank the Connecticut Commission on the Arts for its generous support.

I would also like to thank my mother, Kathy Duval, who, in her own way, taught me how to tell a story.

CONTENTS

FOREWORD

ONCE IN A WHILE a collection of stories comes along that knocks you back, makes you rethink your life, with its daily rhythms, small epiphanies, moments of hope and despair, and glimpses of grandeur. I had that experience when reading *Rear View* by Pete Duval. Here, I thought, is work that moves beyond the easy formulations of criticism. Duval has his own angle on the world, writing with assurance and generosity about ordinary people and the way they move through their lives without flinching, about the way they dream and fuss, fill with unrequited desire, rue the day, absolve themselves, and forgive others.

The opening of "Cellular," for example, breaks with a distinctive, warm freshness: "I'm Frank Lecuyer, seventy-two years old and descended from French kings of the Middle Ages. But that was a long time ago. Nowadays, I live with my wife, Gladys, who's been mentally impaired for fifteen years." This is bathos supreme: from the sublime to the ridiculous, from royal grandeur to the grinding impoverishment of time and sad circumstance. The story continues with a swift, clean narrative that gathers in its confident flow the world's ten thousand objects: "a set of brightly colored plastic trays" or a "plastic patio chair," all the visual cues that conduct us into daily life in our time, where cellular towers rise threateningly, and where birds call from the meadow. It's a world that seems ordinary on the surface, but where secrets and surprises lie in store, such as the five "black plastic contractor's bags crammed full of mail" in the basement of a house, undelivered.

The question of belief rises naturally in the minds of Duval's largely uneducated or unsophisticated characters, who are often seen coming and going to church, to confession, confessing to each other or to a priest. They mostly cannot accept the literal truth of the Catholic faith, but they can't put it away either. When Gilbert in "Midnight Mass" is asked about life after death, his response is typical of Duval's characters: "He's nowhere," he says. "He's a pile of ashes." He says this while eating a fricassee, in a story about a young man whose mother is badly burned in an accident.

An offbeat wryness permeates this and most of these stories, giving them a lively edge. There is an unbridgeable distance between reality and the imagination in the minds of these characters, who generally plod on through the work and play of their lives without much complaint.

"Bakery," a remarkable story, begins with a stunning sense of the world as repetition:

> The first time he saw Red, Gus was leaning against the cooling ovens with some of the other men from his shift, drinking coffee and staring out the six-foot windows of the bakery's third floor. The morning sun squatted on the Fairhaven side of the Acushnet River like a flattened neon ball. Gus had spent sixteen hours feeding cast-iron trays to an antique dough-press machine. His wrists and elbows ached. His lungs were raw. He was still new at the Our Bread Baking Company, still on call, and the night foreman used him wherever and whenever he was needed, sometimes filling in for guys who were sick, sometimes spelling workers during their breaks.

So we meet Red and Gus. We also meet their bakery world, which has not changed much since the height of the Industrial

Revolution; it's a Dickensian world, a version of Dickens's blacking factory—a place where the sensitive soul is crushed, made to fit a dimension of time and space that is uncomfortable but strangely reassuring, as well, in its daily qualities, its lack of pretension. The natural world is measured by this frame, as in the sun that squats "like a flattened neon ball." The writing here, as everywhere in *Rear View*, is matter-of-fact, clean, lucid, fresh.

Readers of this collection will, of course, detect the author's lineage—he has obviously read, admired, and learned a good deal from Raymond Carver and Andre Dubus. But Duval is hardly derivative. His voice is distinctly his own, part of the working-class, Roman Catholic culture it often portrays yet not co-opted by it. The details of American life in the late twentieth century are all here, including the cars, as in the brilliant opening story, "Impala." This tale opens on the move, with Roy and Maysle crossing from Illinois into Missouri. Duval is a poet of the road here, listening closely as the tires "buzzed the gridwork of a bridge spanning wide fields of alfalfa." His eye is sharp as well, unreeling images in a dazzling array. Roy, at forty-two, asks himself the question that seems on the mind of every character in this fiction: *Jesus Christ, what the hell have I been up to for twenty years?*

Duval is, in the end, a religious writer. His view of daily life is sacramental, and the works and days of his characters unfold in a kind of liturgy—in the bakery, in the diner, on the road, at home, in the church. There is a holy hush in the prose at times, as the natural world shines on plastic, on walls, on rooftops, glittering, inviting its people into moments of contemplation, reflection, self-scrutiny, confession, absolution.

Quite fittingly, the collection ends with "Pious Objects," my favorite story in the book, centered on the elderly Father Gaston, who draws only five parishioners—elderly ones, as might be expected—to his morning Mass. On his recent birthday he received a card from a seminary friend who included an obituary from a Montreal newspaper that conveyed the information that a very old teacher had died at ninety-seven. Father Gaston "spent the rest of that day in a kind of glazed reminiscence." On the day during which the story unfolds, he is once again full of memories. It was "the kind of day, he had once remarked to a fellow seminarian, that lent itself to the authentic contemplation of suffering, that made us more aware of it, and of its beauty and rightful place in lives lived for Christ."

So few writers these days have any affection, or understanding, of the religious life. While hardly writing as an advocate of any particular dogma, Duval nevertheless sets before us a world of suffering and pain. He understands that this is the human condition, and that there are also moments of grace, and moments of willed absolution, as at the end of the touching confessional scene that brings "Pious Objects" to a close. Gaston has been told of a defilement of the Blessed Virgin, and his heart is weighed down. "For hours the heaviness stayed with him. It was evening before Father Gaston emerged from the curtained stall of the confessional, long after he had sent the other man out into the world with a clear conscience."

I felt a bit like that after reading, then rereading, this collection. My heart was a little heavy. But I also felt strangely absolved, as if the writer had performed a miraculous service, lightening my conscience, letting me see how I was like everybody else: part of the sad parade, a small figure on the frieze of history, an ordinary man and reader. Pete Duval has given us something very special here. The rearview mirror of his fiction is luminous and wide.

JAY PARINI
Judge, 2003 Bakeless Prize for Fiction

REAR VIEW

Impala

BY MIDAFTERNOON Roy and Maysle Potts were crossing from Illinois into Missouri. The Impala's tires buzzed the gridwork of a bridge spanning wide fields of alfalfa. *New Orleans,* Roy was thinking, *New Orleans, New Orleans.* The rhythm of the words kept time with the *thup* of the expansion joints as the big convertible rocked and bridge girders sent shadows stuttering over him and his wife. "Look," Roy said, pointing. Sometimes he was amazed at the simplest things. It was something for his notebook—the rows of green shimmering below them like a folding fan laid flat in the sun. But Maysle didn't look. She was in the last chapter of a mystery novel and thinking about the fact that they'd been on the road for five hours—since leaving Rockford—and Roy hadn't stopped talking. "Look," he said again. "Cairo, Illinois. Except it's *Kay-row.*" Maysle raised her head for a second. The tight skin of her neck stretched as she peered over the edge of the roadway. She lifted her eyebrows.

"That's nice, Roy." With that she dropped her eyes to the book in her lap. Sometimes she had to use the skills she'd learned in her fifteen years as a court stenographer—the ability to listen without really listening. Roy didn't seem to notice. He didn't notice a lot of things. He kept himself entertained well enough.

"That's some of the best farmland in the world," he said. He was still pointing. "Right there."

Roy drove with his belt unbuckled and the button of his shorts undone. His tank top showed through the white-striped Guayabera shirt he wore, which hung loosely over the roll at his waist. The wind slapped what was left of his blond hair against his forehead. He had a pale, hairless face, as though a white flash of light had singed his eyebrows clean. His eyes moved constantly. He squinted and licked his lips. On his last trip to New Orleans, he'd traveled this same route with Kyle Hoyt and Aloysius McDermott, two of his graduate school friends. They'd come down in Roy's last semester at the University of Illinois, two years before he'd even met Maysle. The three of them took turns at the wheel, driving all night, stopping only to pee and buy beer and eat the baked potatoes and roasted chicken breasts they'd wrapped in aluminum foil and wedged into the crevices of the engine. They'd measured cooking times by the green mile markers.

A little farther into Missouri, Roy said, "I just wish it was going to be Mardi Gras." It was the middle of August, as far from Fat Tuesday as you could get.

"No, you don't," said Maysle.

Roy blew air through his nose. "Yes, I do."

"Mardi Gras is hell, Roy." Sometimes she had to shut him down before he even got going on a topic. She had agreed to drive the fourteen hours to New Orleans, but she at least wanted it to be their trip, not the echo of some time before Roy had even met her.

"How would you know? You've never been."

Maysle folded her finger in the book and turned her green eyes on him. "Hundreds of drunk people having sex in the street?" She wore a sleeveless yellow blouse, a shade or two lighter than the Impala's interior. Her short red hair churned in the breeze. "What's the mystery?"

"Come on, May. Mardi Gras is fun." But the word *fun*—the empty feeling it left behind in the air—seemed to prove Maysle's point. Was anything *fun* anymore?

"That was how long ago?" Maysle asked. "When's the last time you were there?" Tangled in her words was another question: *How long had it been since they'd made love?* They both heard it.

"Nineteen seventy-seven." A Winnebago inched by on their left, shedding a wind that nudged the Impala toward the breakdown lane. Roy was still unsure of the car's handling—the hood was impossibly long. "It was fun, May." Two young boys waved at Roy from the Winnebago's rear window. He lifted two fingers off the wheel.

"People puking into each other's shoes," she said. He clamped his lips down on a smile. She'd remembered his stories. "That's fun?"

"You've never been." He glanced down at the needle of the big speedometer. He was doing seventy-five. "At least I've been, so don't tell me it's not fun."

"And how old were you, Royal?"

He looked over at her. "Twenty-four."

"Twenty-four." She lowered her head to the book again. Roy hated when she did that, when she called up a tone of voice that could end a conversation the way you snap off an icicle. All their discussions seemed to end that way, if not with a cold snap, then with a slack and empty feeling that nothing was ever talked out between them, nothing ever settled. Their discussions about money never changed the way they spent it. Didn't they still live in the same apartment in New Bedford, Massachusetts, that they'd rented for thirteen years? New Bedford! And about kids, the fact that there weren't any—what had come of those tentative discussions? It wasn't a topic Roy liked to think about. Maysle had turned forty-one the month before.

• • •

The Impala belonged to Maysle's newest brother-in-law, Wayne. It was a mint-condition, powder blue, 1971 eight-cylinder convertible with a spotless chrome grill, long bench seats still wrapped in manufacturer's plastic, and a trunk so big Roy imagined you could fit his Escort into it—disassembled, of course. They had driven that Escort out from Massachusetts to visit Maysle's family in Illinois for the wedding.

Roy had never thought of himself as much of a gear head or a car guy—hell, he taught English at a Catholic high school—but he'd almost wet his pants when Wayne rumbled up in the Impala. It was the same model as the car Roy had driven to New Orleans eighteen years earlier. The sun seemed to melt down the curve of the hood. With his hands in his pockets, he asked Wayne if he could take it for a "short jaunt" up Rural Route 10 and back. Maysle rolled her eyes and leveled at Roy a look he tried to ignore. He and Wayne had barely been introduced, and Roy wanted to take off in the man's car? "Sure," Wayne said, though his grimace said something else. He was a tax attorney. He collected vintage automobiles, kept them in a brick warehouse in downtown Rockford. He threw Roy the keys. "Knock yourself out." Watching Roy pull away, Maysle wanted to apologize. *He's like a child sometimes,* she almost said. But what came out of her mouth was, "I wouldn't worry, Wayne. He'll bring it back in one piece. He's very careful."

"No problem," said Wayne.

In some things, Maysle knew, Roy could be too careful. There was that time they'd been out to visit her parents for Christmas seven years earlier. One night, in the bathroom, she'd heard her father through the bedroom wall. "Are they ever going to have kids? It's like they're goddamn roommates." Maysle climbed back into bed with Roy and woke him, his eyes snapping open when she reached up under his boxers and cupped his balls in her cold palm. He climbed on top of her, and it was so forbidden and kinky with her parents only a few yards away. There were no more condoms in his shaving case, and he just would not let himself go inside her without one. "Come on," she whispered, grinding her hips against his the way she knew he loved it. But he held on. How could he be that careful—with her, his wife? What the hell was he thinking about? She'd been just as unsure about having kids as Roy had, but she had always thought at some point they'd just let go and leave it to chance. Isn't that what married people did? And now it was too late. When she'd begun to skip her periods, she'd seen a doctor. It started earlier for some women. But she hadn't told Roy yet. She didn't know how to tell him.

Alone now out on the nameless farm roads, Roy jammed his sneaker to the Impala's floor panel. The gravel flew, and pigs and chickens scrambled pell-mell back from barbed-wire fences. "Lordy," Roy kept saying. "Oh, m' lordy." The dashboard was a dream, all buffed stainless steel and substantial. He kept snapping the radio on and off, the knobs sparkling in the afternoon light. He jacked up the brakes and skidded to a stop in the sand near an irrigation ditch. He lowered the roof and looked around. He got out of the car and shut the door and tucked in his shirt. Then he walked backward across the road, measuring his steps as he went. He stood for a moment, admiring the automobile from this short distance. He looked left and then right. "Go!" he said, and he ran, his belly jiggling, and jumped over the door into the front seat. He slammed the transmission into gear. The wheels wrapped themselves in gray clouds of burnt rubber as the car fishtailed. The tires caught the asphalt with a screech. "Lordy, lordy."

Two hours later, at the end of his in-laws' long driveway, he hitched up his pants while the engine ticked itself cool. The sun had gone down, but the sky was still light. *I'm forty-two years old,* he thought. *Jesus Christ, what the hell have I been up to for twenty years?* And right there he made up his mind: *Maysle will just have to deal with it. It'll be good for us.* He ignored the little belch of shame that burned at the top of his throat. *What the hell do I ever ask of her?* Then he turned and walked into the kitchen, where Maysle and her parents and sisters and nephews and Wayne sat around the table eating large fatty sandwiches. When Maysle saw his face, she knew exactly what was in his mind. His mouth had that toothless, puckered look. She wondered what it would do when she told him the news.

Wayne stretched a smile. "Here he is," he said. Maysle's sister Mavis, Wayne's fiancée, had one arm around his neck. She was feeding him a dill pickle spear with the other. "Where the hell have you been?"

Roy stood in the doorway, trying to look as serious as he could. He'd hooked his thumbs in his belt loops — he didn't know exactly why. He waited for everyone to stop talking. Then he said, "I want to buy it."

"Sorry, it's not for sale," Wayne said. "Sorry, buddy."

"I want to buy it, Wayne. I want to drive that car from here to New Orleans." Maysle's mother laughed, her freckled hands screening a mouthful of food. "I'm serious, Wayne. What'll you take for it?"

"You don't want it, believe me," said Wayne. "It's a nutbreaker to keep up and running."

"What'll you take?"

"Royal." Maysle's eyes were hard and round. "Have we talked about New Orleans?"

That tone, Roy thought. But he was way out ahead of her. Yes, they had talked about New Orleans. Many times over the years. "What'll you take, Wayne? Name it."

Wayne shook his head as though he'd caught a whiff of something rank. He let out a long breath. His future in-laws were watching him. Mavis stopped twisting his hair around her pinky. "How long are you going to be gone?"

"A week." Roy's scalp itched with longing.

"Roy," Maysle said. "We have a car."

Roy tried to match the hardness of her gaze. "You want to drive into New Orleans in a damn Ford Escort?" He turned back to Wayne.

"Tell you what," Wayne said. "You can rent it from me." At that the small children in the room sent up a little cheer for

Uncle Roy, then fell to the linoleum, squealing and writhing on their heels and elbows.

"All right." Roy was grinning foolishly. "It'll be here when you get back from Saint Croix."

After sloping away from the Mississippi River, Interstate 57 straightened into a corridor of factories and industrial parks. Maysle finished her novel. She'd been sitting on her calves. She held the book shut in her two hands for a moment and looked out her side of the car. Smoke jetted from stacks that gleamed in the afternoon sunlight like organ pipes, some of them tufted with flames. She put the novel in the back seat.

"Good book?" Roy asked. He'd been quiet for a while. Somewhere along this stretch eighteen years ago Kyle Hoyt had asked him to take over at the wheel. "Let's switch without stopping," Kyle Hoyt said. Aloysius McDermott wheezed a laugh, his face gathering up around his nose—but they'd done it. They'd bumped and slid and tumbled as the headlights raked across four empty lanes. A few minutes later Roy was driving, and Kyle Hoyt lay in the back seat. They hadn't been below sixty miles per hour.

Maysle nodded. "Yeah, not bad. But these plots get a little old."

"Any, ah, sexy stuff in there?"

Maysle looked at him sideways. "A little, Roy."

"Anything you'd want to share?"

"Well, a couple of people do it in an attic."

"Wow," he said. "The nasty in an attic."

"The what?"

"You've never heard of the nasty?"

"Never."

"It seems to be a big part of my students' vocabulary."

"Really."

"Yeah. Fifteen, and they're already well acquainted with the nasty."

Maysle tried the word out. Roy laughed.

"A good name for it, huh?" he said.

She looked at him blankly. Did he already know? She should have hated him, but she didn't. She loved him. Or was it something closer to sympathy at that moment?

"What do you think?" he asked. "The nasty. Doing the nasty. Getting jiggy."

She laughed, but she was feeling a little woozy. It had been coming for a long time. She made up her mind. He had to know. "Roy, we need to talk about something."

The car moved halfway into the next lane as he made a pantomime of looking for someone in the back seat. "It's just us here, May," he said, facing forward. "It's always been just us. What's on your mind?"

"Roy."

"Wait," he said. "You going to answer my question first?"

"What about?"

"The nasty, May. About doing the nasty."

"What about it?"

"I think the kids have it down—their name for it." He was feeling his way along the contours of something—what, he didn't exactly know. "Do you like that name?"

"It's never been nasty between us, Roy."

After a pause, he said, "I've never thought so, either."

For a mile or two, Maysle didn't say anything.

"So you want to talk," he said. "Where do we start? Can we start with the question of the year?"

"Which is?"

"See, this is the whole point—we can never get down to it."

"What?" she said. "Why haven't we had sex in a year?"

He gave the horn a blast. "Now we're talking turkey. I knew this trip would be good for us."

They drove on for a while with the sound of the wind whistling past the side mirrors.

"I have to use a restroom, Roy."

"Yeah, me too."

The highway had curved back toward the Mississippi River, cutting through fields of corn and soybean. They passed two more exits before Roy veered the car down an off-ramp and onto a long strip of Best Westerns, Taco Bells, and car dealerships. In the tighter traffic, the Impala handled like a sled.

Roy backed into the corner of a McDonald's parking lot and shut off the ignition, the wheels straddling the yellow line between spaces. "You go first," he said. His voice had softened. "I don't want to leave the car alone." She smiled and reached over to touch his face.

"I love you, Roy," she said. He nipped feebly at her fingers. As she walked to the restaurant, he sat with the door open, his legs straight out, watching his wife. Just beneath her navy blue culottes, the hollows of her knees looked sinewy and dry in the afternoon light. She had such spidery forearms, so fragile. Roy reached under his seat and pulled out a small green notebook with a pen jammed into the wire binding. For years he'd kept a running list of notes and observations, though he wasn't exactly sure why anymore. Someday he'd need them. That much he knew. Five years before, he'd published a short story in a little Midwestern college magazine. If he could only face his material squarely, he knew he could write something as good again —he just needed some material to face. So he took notes. He rarely read them over, surprised as he always was at how stupid they could sound days and weeks later. Sometimes he crossed out a line in a rush of embarrassment, though he knew that no one, not even Maysle, would ever read them.

He pulled off the elastic band and flipped through the sheets, looking for the first clean page. He read: *Greyhound with clipped tail. Lemon sunlight on the Dress Barn. Boy walking with limp. Seventeen years old—a shivering blade after rain.* He paused over that one—that was Katya Johansson. Besides teaching English at the high school, Roy coached winter track, girls and boys. He would hover at the doorway to the girls' locker room, using a tongue depressor to pick clumps of sod out of the cleats of the tight track shoes he wore, and waiting for Katya to emerge in her plaid skirt and button-down Oxford shirt after her shower. When she passed in front of a window, sometimes he could make out the silhouette of her breasts and stomach.

A few pages further on, there was a list of names he'd found in phone books or overheard in conversation—for fictional characters—and a diagram for a bookcase he'd never made. Then, not completely scratched out: *English department meeting Friday—Robert's Rules of Ogre.* He slid down in the seat and wrote: *seventeen years old—a soft place behind the knees.* He wondered how squarely Maysle could face his material. The heat from the blacktop rose in waves that blurred a Ponderosa Steakhouse sign across the street. He told himself he would take a lot of notes in New Orleans.

When Maysle walked out through the glass doors, he snapped the elastic band back in place and slid the notebook under his seat. He stepped out of the car and buttoned his shorts. They touched hands as they passed each other, and he walked into the cool air of the restaurant. Roy had always had trouble peeing in public places, so he was glad to have the men's restroom to himself. In the past, whenever someone pushed through the door behind him, he would feel all naked and vulnerable and lean in against the urinal. His prostate would seem to seize up like a blood pressure cuff, and no matter how long he stood there, wagging his pecker by a pinch of loose skin, nothing happened. Then he'd have to pretend to finish off, squaring his shoulders and shamming a little post-piss shake before zipping up and walking back out to the car to suffer until the next stop. He could hold it in so long it sometimes scared him. On his last trip to New Orleans he'd driven for hours with his bladder swollen and his hand in his crotch before he asked Kyle Hoyt and Aloysius McDermott to pull over on a Mississippi interstate so he could run up into the scrub pines.

Out in the car, Maysle leaned back in the seat and looked up at the light post they'd parked under. She didn't want to ruin New Orleans for Roy. She didn't want him to feel the way she felt. This must be the way some women were about getting pregnant, she thought—scared what the words would finally do to their lives. But in her case, instead of there being one thing more to talk about, there'd be one thing less.

Roy walked over to the car. Leaning on her door, he asked Maysle if she were hungry. He felt good, his bladder light and empty. "Not really," she said.

"Well, I'm going to get a little something," he said. She watched him walk around the car and get in. He turned the key and revved the engine.

"You're going to use the drive-through?"

"Sure."

"You were just inside the restaurant."

He pulled away from the curb, the wheel turning sluggishly under his hands. His mouth had that toothless, puckered look again.

"That's dumb, Roy."

"What? I just want to see the face on the window cashier when I pull up in this car."

"That's ridiculous," she said.

"Why?"

"Let's just go in and eat if you're hungry."

"You don't like the way I've been driving? You don't think I can handle this bus?" He patted the side of the door.

"Roy."

"Like threading a needle, baby," he said. He squeezed her knee. "Not a problem."

He circled the parking lot so he could enter the drive-through lane straight on, but even then the big nose of the Impala wouldn't make the turn. "Easy," he said. "No problem." He threw the car into reverse, eased back, and tried again. This time he made the first turn of the lane, and they pulled up to the menu board. "See?" Maysle couldn't help smiling. He asked for a large order of french fries and edged the car forward. But at the second corner the left front tire jumped the curb and rolled over a line of red tulips.

"Oh, God, Royal," said Maysle. When the driver behind them

gave a blast on his horn, Roy felt the dryness of his tongue. He crept the corner of the bumper forward, and the front end came down with a horrific scrape that seemed to register somewhere behind his testicles. He patted Maysle's knee. His hand was shaking.

"No sweat, May."

"You're unbelievable."

A Little League baseball team had gathered behind the tinted glass of the restaurant. They were laughing and pounding the window with the heels of their hands. Up ahead, the cashier leaned out the side of the building with her headset and microphone on. "Back it, back it," she was saying. They could hear her over the intercom. "Don't come any farther, sir. Back it." But there was no backing out of the lane now. Roy knew he'd come too far. He tapped the pedal, testing the edge of the curb against the back tire. There was some resistance. Then he gave it a little gas, and the car surged up on the curb again and forward into the brick pillar of the drive-through portico. "The goddamn lane's just too narrow," Roy said.

"That's right, Roy."

He shifted into neutral and let the engine idle. He couldn't open his door far enough to get out. They were wedged in. Then he remembered it was a convertible and stood up on the seat, his hands on his hips. The driver behind him leaned on the horn again. Roy sat on the backrest and pretended to ponder the situation, but his mind was beyond reason. He slid down and shut the door. He shifted into drive. "What are you doing?" The window cashier's voice was loud enough to hear without the microphone now. "Stop."

"Will you shut the hell up?" Roy yelled. He wrenched the wheel and stutter-stepped the gas pedal, his left sneaker on the brake, and there was a sound like a sob as the front bumper squeezed past the first column, taking a brick with it, and edged into the light on the far side of the portico. Roy's face felt stiff as he got out of the car and walked around to Maysle's side. Two ragged grooves ran the length of the Impala, pinching the reflection of Roy's chubby legs to a bright line in the blue metal. The handle to Maysle's door was gone. The right side rearview mirror lay in the middle of the drive-through lane like a crumpled bird. When the cashier came out of the restaurant, she picked up the mirror and dropped it in the bag with Roy's order of french fries.

Driving farther south, they didn't speak for half an hour. An orange sun rode the horizon behind black clumps of trees that seemed to rush out from the highway to the far end of the fields and back again. The Impala kept fading to the right. If Roy turned the wheel too far in the other direction, he felt a thumping under his palms. Maysle hadn't noticed, and he wasn't going to point it out to her. He angled the car into a rest area to put up the roof. Then he got out of the car to look at the damage again. Knowing Maysle's eyes were on him, he tried to give his step a cheerful little hop. But he knew what was coming. He got back into the car.

"I think we should turn around," Maysle said, finally. "As far as I'm concerned, the trip is over."

"Why?" Roy's voice sounded too high. He coughed into this fist. "We haven't even gotten to Memphis."

"We don't have a door handle on my side."

"That's no big deal, Maysle."

She looked off into the trees. She knew what might make him turn back. She could feel the words, raw and hot in her throat now.

"When we get to Beale Street, we'll eat a plate of gumbo," he said. "You'll feel better."

"I don't like gumbo. Never have."

"Well, I'll feel better, then."

"Roy, let's go back to Illinois." Maysle was thinking of her sisters' kids. She wanted to hear them lisp her name.

"Look, Wayne's a lawyer, right?" Roy accelerated back onto the highway. "He's a smart guy. He'll have insurance."

"You're going to be one of his favorites."

"What do you want me to do? Call the Virgin Islands to tell him we scratched the finish?"

"Scratched the finish?" she said.

"That? That's nothing to a car guy like Wayne."

On the beltway around Memphis Roy nudged Maysle awake. They'd been driving for hours. "We're here," he said. He pointed to a cluster of tall buildings, the windows a checkerboard of pale blue lights against the night sky. At the bottom of an exit they merged onto another stretch of strip malls and chain restaurants. Rows of overhead traffic signals rocked in the wind. Roy drove into the parking lot of an EconoLodge and looked over at Maysle. "Is this OK?"

"Yeah, but do me a favor, Roy." When she tried her door, it wouldn't open. She turned in her seat, braced herself against his arm, and kicked the handle with the heel of her shoe. The door shuddered on its hinge.

"I'm impressed."

"Just don't try to drive under the breezeway."

"Not a problem."

Waiting in the car, Roy noticed a sign in crooked block lettering welcoming participants of the Evinrude Outboard Golf Tournament. He could see Maysle talking to the woman at the desk. She was smiling and nodding, but when she turned to walk out, the smile left her face. "No vacancy," she said, slamming the door.

"No room at the inn, huh?"

Maysle didn't say anything.

They drove farther along the strip, stopping at each motel they saw, but every time Maysle went in, she came right back out. "The golf tournament's loaded them solid." Her face had tightened. Her voice had begun to rasp. "We should have called ahead, Roy."

"Hey, I realize this."

She turned in her seat and looked him directly in the face. She was wondering how hard she'd have to hit him to break his nose. "You're not twenty-four anymore."

"Right," he said.

"I'm sure as hell not sleeping in the car."

They got back on the interstate and headed west across the Mississippi River into Arkansas. The woman at the Holiday Inn had told Maysle they would have an easier time finding a room in West Memphis. Roy leaned forward as he drove, his eyes squinting over the steering wheel. Maysle wedged herself into the far corner of the long seat. She was watching the yellow lines. She and Roy seemed to move down a tunnel carved out of the night by their headlights, the beams crisscrossed by moths and gnats. It was almost an hour before they saw another cluster of motels and gas stations. In the parking lot of a shabby Ramada Inn, Maysle slammed the door especially hard and stamped her way to the entrance. If it weren't for her, she was thinking, where the hell would Roy be? Didn't he need her more than she needed him?

Roy watched her walk to the vestibule, her arms around her ribs. The farther away she got, the harder it was to tell she was his wife. *What would happen if I just left her here and drove off?* The bottom of his lungs seemed to clutch at the thought of it. He imagined living by himself in New Orleans. In the French Quarter, in a small second-floor room with a balcony and those wrought-iron railings. They needed English teachers everywhere, didn't they? He shook his head briskly and rubbed his burning eyes. He didn't know how much farther he could drive.

On the other side of a chainlink fence, six or seven teenage kids chased each around the pool in wet tuxedos and satin dresses, their bare feet slapping the concrete. There was an explosion of water and then laughter. Maysle walked quickly out of the foyer and over to the car. She dangled a room key in front of him. "All they had was a room for smokers," she said. "I made an executive decision."

"Fine with me."

Nighthawks screeched above the orange buzz of the parking lot lights as Roy popped the trunk. He carried the luggage up the cement steps, the shouts and laughter from the pool echoing off the walls. When he opened the door, he saw himself and Maysle silhouetted in the mirror at the back of the room. The air smelled of soggy cigars. He snapped on the lights. There were cigarette burns in the olive carpeting. "Oh, Christ," he said.

"I don't care." Maysle staggered over and fell onto the bed. Still in her clothes, she toed her sneakers off and wormed herself underneath the bedspread.

"Are you going to sleep like that?"

"Yes, sir. I sure as hell am."

"I'm not." Roy took off his shorts and unbuttoned the white-striped Cuban shirt. In his boxers and tank top, he brushed his teeth at the mirror. After rinsing his mouth, he stood back and looked at how wide his hips had gotten. *Goddamn.* He clasped his hands behind him and straightened his elbows as far as he could. *I've got no chest anymore.* Then he went over and parted the curtain. The light played in chops on the surface of the pool. A tall boy wearing only a dinner jacket and briefs sat with his arms around two girls in their ruined dresses. They were slapping at his hands and laughing. Roy would have taken some notes on what he saw, but his notebook was still under the seat of the Impala.

Lying on her side, Maysle thought of how the doctor had told her the news. She'd known what he was going to say, but it was different with the words finally out there in the brightness of the examination room. It was very different. Now she was weaving in and out of sleep. *Tomorrow,* she thought. *You're going to have to know tomorrow, Roy. I'm sorry. We're heading back to Rockford in the morning.*

Roy sat in the chair next to the bed. He thought he heard something on the other side of the wall. He got up and pressed his ear to a patch of wallpaper above the television. Was that a woman panting in the next room? It sounded like someone making love in there. He listened until his neck cramped up. It was all part of his research and observation, he told himself. He just didn't have his notebook handy. He had to get his materials down, didn't he?

He pulled back the covers of the bed and got in gently, one leg at a time. Maysle was sleeping between the sheets and the spread. He nestled his stomach up to her, his knees at the warm backs of hers. *New Orleans,* Roy was thinking. *If we drive all day tomorrow, we can make it by nightfall.*

Wheatback

T HE ELEVATOR slowed at the second floor, hesitated, then stopped. The doors opened unevenly. Paul stepped out, gripping the flowers he'd bought. They were wrapped in a cone of paper that crackled loudly whenever he shifted his moist hands. It was his first visit to the nursing home since his father had been moved there. He did not know the name of the flowers. They were large and expensive, and they looked like birds. They would do.

After the accident, Paul's father had been attended to by a private nurse who came to the house twice a day—midmorning, midafternoon. She kept up a rhythm with Paul's mother so that his father would never be alone for more than an hour or so. In the afternoons, coming home from school, Paul would meet the nurse on her way out. Mrs. Nordstrom. She seemed nice enough—mild and hefty. She always had something pleasant to say, little things. She asked Paul about school, or talked about the weather or the Red Sox. Over the months Paul grew to enjoy seeing Mrs. Nordstrom. Their brief chat was for him a last breath of air until he emerged for school the next morning. But when the money ran out and she simply stopped coming, Paul convinced himself that he had hated her all along.

The floor was empty. The hallway smelled of dirty laundry and stale food. From a window at the far end, the fall of late afternoon light on the cracked linoleum showed patches of dust the mops had missed. *Holidays,* his mother had always called them. Paul walked to the nursing station. Two green lamps shone on a stack of files, loose papers falling out all over the desk. He thought he heard a TV somewhere on the floor—a soft and comforting sound, the music from *Jeopardy!* He began to move slowly along the corridor. From a dark room to his left, someone called to him: "Boy!" He stopped suddenly, almost dropping the flowers. "Way past visiting hours, fella."

Paul began to speak in the direction of the voice, to explain why he was late. He had an after-school job now, and he needed the hours. But the voice interrupted him.

"Come on in here." The voice sounded peeved and impatient. Paul edged toward the open door. He couldn't see who had spoken the words to him. In the room the TV babbled to itself, the sound turned down low. Flickering blue light crawled and jerked everywhere.

"Do you know where room 202 is?" Paul asked, smiling nervously into the shifting blue shadows. Like an icon, the TV was mounted high in the corner of the room.

"Come on in, boy," said the voice, "and close the door."

Paul stepped into the room. "I'm kind of late."

"Close the door." Neither male nor female, the voice rose weak and thin like cigarette smoke in the blue darkness.

"What room number is this?"

"Close the door, boy."

Paul slowly closed the wide door behind him, leaving it slightly ajar. The paper cone of flowers crackled in his hand. In the corner opposite the TV was a bed with chrome railings along the sides. Something small lay under a thin but freshly draped sheet. *Jeopardy!* ended in a whisper of applause, and the drums and trumpets of the evening news filled the room.

"They say always leave the door open, but the hell with them," the voice said. Paul's eyes began to adjust to the darkness of the room. "Nobody out there, anyway." Paul shifted the flowers from one hand to the other. "Maybe they're on strike. Who the hell knows?"

"There was no one at the desk," Paul offered, pointing with the flowers toward the door.

"Don't think there's ever *been* anyone at the desk, boy." The voice slowed over Paul's words with a shade of mockery. "Anyway." The voice feebly tried to clear itself. "So what do you want to talk about?"

Paul's skin was getting hot and crawly. "I really can't stay long. I'm not even supposed to —"

"Boy." The lumps and tiny valleys under the sheet shifted a little. "How old are you?"

Paul hesitated, wondering whether he should answer. "Seventeen."

"Seventeen!" The voice sounded out of breath. "How many times does seventeen go into a hundred and four?"

"Is that how old you are?" Paul asked. Things were getting weird, but he would have an interesting story to tell Jennifer when he called her that night.

"Maybe I'm just interested in your division skills, boy." The voice seemed to smile, though Paul couldn't really see for sure. "Yes. As of last Monday — one hundred and four years old."

Paul knew how women acted when the topic of age came up in conversation. He remembered asking Mrs. Lavesque how old she was one day while she and some of his mother's other friends sipped tea at the kitchen table, a simple question, and how everything seemed to explode and all eyes fell on him and people laughed and mussed his hair and pretend-slapped his face.

"Pretty well along, huh, boy?" The voice changed, a quavering like the effect on a candle flame when someone passes by. "Now ask me how long I been in here." Paul waited. "Go ahead. Ask me how long I been in this place."

"How long have you been in this place?"

"How many times does seventeen go into twenty-seven?"

Paul said, "Wow."

"Same room, same bed," said the voice slowly, as if hanging the wet words out to dry in the stale blue air of the room. Paul leaned back against a wall. The flowers hung limp now in his hand. "Sit down, boy, will you? There's a chair by the door there."

It was getting very late. Paul began to speak. He had to go. His father was probably already asleep, and he'd missed his chance to see him that night. But again the voice interrupted.

"Sit down."

Paul sat down.

"You watch the news?"

Paul looked up at the TV. "Sometimes, with my father." He imagined his father's speechless gaze, the dance of color reflected in the moistness there.

The voice whispered: "You done it yet, boy?"

Paul paused before speaking. "Done what?"

"You got a girlfriend?" the voice said quietly. Peter Jennings talked about the West Bank, about how many Palestinians had been killed that day.

"Yeah, I have a girlfriend."

"Well, then, what I'm asking is, have you, you know, done it, with your girlfriend?" The sentence trailed off into the noise of the television.

Paul motioned to get up, but he stopped, knees bent, and sat back down. "Yeah, I've done it." At school, in the corridors, in the locker room after track, he had often listened to the other boys snapping phrases like towels at each other — "pussy," "piece of ass." But he'd always held himself aloof, and no one had ever pressed him to talk about anything like sex.

He felt an excitement that verged on shame.

The voice now rose to full volume: "Then tell me all about it, boy."

Paul smiled and shook his head in the darkness. "No," he

said. "You tell me first if you've ever done it." And after a pause the voice began to crackle like the cone of flowers, slowly at first, then building into a rapid, phlegm-choked chuckle, lewd and out of control, and ending in a harsh cough. Between breaths the voice tried to speak.

"Boy—"

"What?" Paul laughed nervously. "What's so funny?"

"I'm one hundred four years of age."

Paul's chest glowed hotly. "Well, if you haven't done it *yet*—" And the voice erupted again with something like "hoooop!" and settled back to hacking. Paul was laughing, too. He couldn't help it.

"I've done it, boy," said the voice when it had gained control again, "but not for a whole long time." Paul looked down at his feet in the dark. "Last time I done it—hey, you live in Fairhaven?"

"Yeah," said Paul.

"All your life?"

"Yeah."

"Me, too." The voice paused while a pretty woman on television talked about deodorant. "There used to be trolley cars in Fairhaven. I bet you didn't know that."

"I've heard about them," Paul said. He put the flowers on the floor by his feet.

"They used to come down along Main Street from up north, swing over, and follow Green Street to Fort Phoenix." The familiar street names sounded strange coming from the voice like that. "Put it this way: the last time I did it, boy, I took a trolley home."

Paul asked, just ahead of a snicker, "What about this person you did it with?" He was still unsure about the voice, whether it belonged to a man or a woman. He knew it was a stupid question.

"Dead."

"Oh," said Paul.

"Now what about you, boy? Let's hear it. Give me the details."

Paul took a deep breath. "There's nothing much to tell." He felt a little guilty, sitting there, as though it were something to be ashamed of. "We do it in my car usually."

"Where?"

"Pope's Island. West Island, mostly. Sometimes the Fort."

"What kind of car do you drive?" The voice sounded impatient.

"Toyota, why?" Paul heard footsteps pass in the hall outside.

"Toyota. What model? Is it a small car? Is it cramped?"

"Yeah, very," Paul said. "Sometimes when no one's home at her house, we go there."

"I understand." The voice paused. "Now back to the car, boy. Front seat or back?"

"Back, mostly."

"I see," said the voice, trailing off again.

Paul felt awkward in the long silence that followed. He considered getting up and walking out of the room. But he didn't. "So what else do you want to know about it?" The words rose to his throat as though of their own volition.

The voice began again immediately, asking about the girl's hair—long or short? blond?—about her size—a big girl? full figured? big in the chest?

"She's small," said Paul. "Not big—"

"And you like it that way, don't you?" the voice said, cutting Paul off again.

Paul shrugged in the dark.

"And how does she like it?" the voice asked.

"Like what?"

"What are we talking about here? It. How does she like it? Up front? From behind?"

"Yes." Paul smiled.

"'Yes' what, boy? Don't leave me hanging. You're killing me." The voice laughed. Then everything got silent again, except for the TV. Peter Jennings's face talked about the person of the week. Who would it be? "Come over here." The voice sounded deadly serious now, dry and stark in the vacant room. "Come here, boy. Something here for you." Paul sat very still. He felt his heart pulsing in his ears. But then, slowly, he stood up and began moving toward the bed. "No more about your girl. What's her name?"

"Jennifer."

"No more about Jennifer. Just come here, and I'll let you go."

Paul heard a snap, and the TV blinked off, leaving a white dot in the center of the screen. Now the room was almost completely dark.

"Um, now I can't see," Paul said, reaching for the wall.

"Follow my voice, boy. I'll keep talking, and you follow it." Paul moved in the direction of the voice, his hand out ahead of him and sweeping across his path in slow, uneasy arcs. For a second, it was like being with Jennifer at night in the car. Then his hand lightly brushed something and reversed its direction and traced backward and touched it again. He closed his hand around two fingers. They felt moist and delicate, like the skin of a boiled chicken, like the lips of a sleeping person. He thought of Jennifer again. "There," said the voice, softer, but much closer this time, almost a whisper. Paul giggled faintly. Then another hand turned Paul's palm upward and held it unsteadily. He let his fingers go slack and tried to concentrate on what he felt, but he couldn't keep it all straight. It was nothing like embarrassment.

"Boy, you take this." Paul felt the fingers press something into his palm, press it firmly there like a brand, and two hands closed his fingers in upon themselves. "This is from the last time I did it." Paul stood still, waiting until the hands released his fist. "I found it on the way home — heads up, boy." Then the voice was silent. Paul still heard the breathing, though, heard it fade as he backed away, turned, and made his way toward where he believed the door was. The flowers crackled under his boot. Bending over, he groped for them. He opened the door, looking backward quickly into the dark room, and in a moment was outside in the muted light of the hallway.

He waited till he could see by the red light of an EXIT sign at the top of the stairwell to look at what he held tight in his fist.

By now, he knew, his father would be sleeping, deep in a private cocoon of tranquilizers and dreams. He glanced along the dark hallway. The nursing station still went unattended. Then he opened his hand slowly. But it was just a penny. He turned it over in the dim light. 1955. A wheatback, edges worn sharp as a paring knife. Worthless.

Midnight Mass

I T WAS Christmas Eve, and Father Bluteau seemed to be looking at me across a brown carpet of parishioners' heads. It must have been my imagination, because he didn't know me from Adam. I stood on one of the steps leading up to the organ loft at the back of the church, steadying myself against the walls of the stairwell, trying to follow his homily; but the whole place—marble columns, blue barrel ceiling, and all— was tilting up and sliding away. Just below me, Johnny Dumas seesawed on his heels. When Father Bluteau said something about the night being "an occasion of joy and celebration," I nudged Johnny in the back of the knee with my boot, and his leg buckled. "So, we got a little jump on the action," I whispered over his shoulder. He tried to elbow me and almost fell into an old lady wearing a red and green kerchief. She held a long silver rosary, and when she looked up at me with her black eyes, I leaned back and made off I was listening to the priest's words. She was still staring when I looked again, her eyes round and black. Shrugging, I mouthed the word *what?* My shoulder caught the plaster foot of a statue of Joseph on a small metal shelf next to my head, and the whole thing pitched forward and started shaking.

Earlier that night, me and Johnny Dumas had driven up and down Acushnet Avenue in his Mustang for hours, drinking lukewarm Narragansett from a case in the back seat and calling for women on street corners to get into the car with us. Two did, and we parked under I-195 for a while. But Johnny's girl started crying for some reason, and the other one called me something nasty in Portuguese, and they both whined until we let them out. Passing St. Anthony's Church again, I let my head loll back on the window to watch the black spire spoke by against the stars, and I got a glimpse at the rows of people through the door. My stomach seized up. I looked at my watch. "Shit, Johnny," I said. "We got to go to midnight Mass." I hadn't been to church in a long time, but the service tonight was being offered for my father. He'd died the year before. Johnny didn't have to know I'd promised my mother I'd be there, and I didn't have to receive Communion. I just had to show up.

Johnny pulled on the brim of the gray fedora he always wore when he drove. "Are you for fucking real?" We worked together at the bakery on Purchase Street. He was just a dumb, fat Canuck like me. He'd put up a fuss about something, but press him hard enough on it, and he'd turn around and say OK. We got along fine.

"Just let me out here," I said.

"Gil, we're shitfaced. Go tomorrow."

"I'm going tonight." I'd already opened the door. When he pulled up to the curb, the front wheel jumped the sidewalk. He shut off the ignition, and we got out. The air felt sharp on my face. I swallowed a few cold breaths and started up the granite steps. Johnny was right behind me, swearing to himself.

We were late. The priest had just begun the Gospel reading. In the vestibule, an old guy in a brown suit crossed his forehead, lips, and chest with his thumbnail, then handed me a bulletin. He looked annoyed. I wondered if he could tell I was buzzing. I smiled and tried to dip a little holy water, but my finger came up dry. I crossed myself anyways, genuflected without falling down, and pushed through knots of men in damp wool overcoats.

Once I'd found a place on the stairs, I searched the pews for my mother. I picked out her hat—her navy blue pillbox with the white netting and fake pearls. She was sitting with her sister, my Aunt Yvonne, close to the aisle, about midway between me and the altar. Good, I thought. Proof of purchase. I could tell her where they'd sat.

Father Bluteau kissed the Bible that the two altar boys were struggling to hold up and walked over to the lectern to start his homily. After a while, Johnny stopped rocking. He was slumped against the door of the confessional with his arms crossed, his chin on his chest. He might have been asleep. I thought I'd give him some shit about it later. Johnny was always giving it to me whenever he could, because I was twenty-two and still living at home. We'd be driving in the Mustang or slamming shots at the Ferry Cafe, and all of a sudden he'd smile in the middle of the point I was making. I knew the next words out of his lips: *mama's boy.* But he had no idea what it was like to live with her—all her talk about Jesus and forgiveness. She believed the Virgin Mary was appearing to ten-year-old peasant kids in Europe who could stare into candle flames for hours and walk backward over rocky terrain without falling. "Conversion, Gilbert. Do you hear what I'm talking about?" my mother would say during the six o'clock news. "The world's coming to pieces." Every earthquake was a sign to her. Freak weather meant the Lord was kicking ass because of abortion. I'd laugh and wave her off, tell her she'd been drinking too much. But even though I couldn't accept any of it—not God or Jesus or the bodily assumption of Mary into heaven—I still couldn't put any of it away, either.

"So if you don't believe," she said one night, "where do you think your father is?" The question had been coming for a long time. We were sitting in front of the TV, eating supper off rickety tin trays.

"You really want to know?"

She nodded. Her eyes were nervous. My father hadn't been a very good Catholic.

"He's nowhere," I said. I swallowed a bite of the fricassee she'd heated up from the night before. "He's a pile of ashes."

"Oh, Gil. You can't believe that."

I nodded with my mouth full.

"I just don't believe you believe that."

"Jesus Christ, Ma." I dropped my fork. "What do you want me to say?" Her burns had started to itch. When she got excited, she'd be scratching. "I'd be happy if he was in heaven, but I just can't see it. It's all a fairy tale."

What bothered me most, though, was the possibility that she didn't believe all that stuff either—not deep down, not really. She wanted to hear me argue because it gave her a chance to convince herself. But I never pushed my side all that hard. I'd ask her about the Buddhists, where they were going when they died—big softball questions like that. I never held up what I knew she was helpless to argue against: that she'd been burned and that I was her son. How could God let these things happen to her?

The Profession of Faith rose around me in a murmur that sounded more like the humming of machinery at the bakery than human voices. A couple of times the old lady with the kerchief looked at me with her black eyes, her mouth moving like she was chewing overdone meat. I moved my own mouth to the words I remembered—the rhythm gave me clues. And then a deacon stood at the lectern and read the General Intercession. He asked us to pray for the Church and the Pope and the bishops and for world peace. And after a long list of names, I heard my father's. It sounded sad and empty coming out of a stranger's mouth like that.

Six months after my father died, I was out with Johnny Dumas. Home alone, my mother put some hair removal wax in a saucepan and set it on the stove. She got into the shower. It was part of her weekly routine. When she turned off the water, she smelled the burning wax and stumbled toward the kitchen with just a towel around her. She stopped in the door frame, stunned by the heavy smell and the sight of those flames. A column of smoke blackened the ceiling above the stove. Whenever I thought about it, I'd see the whole thing from above, with nothing to do but watch as she pulled the towel from around her body and waved it over the pan. The corner of the towel caught the handle, the pan flipped up, and my mother was spattered with the hot wax. She staggered into the living room, knocking over a floor lamp, screaming, and pulling out handfuls of her hair. She tripped out into the stairwell. Mrs. Pacheco, our downstairs neighbor, had heard the screams. She trapped my mother in her arms on the second-floor landing and pushed her back up the stairs and into the shower again. Under the hot water, they scraped the wax away before it hardened. Her skin came off with the wax.

When I got to the hospital, she was lying under a sheet propped up with poles, like a Red Cross tent. Her face looked splashed with white paint. Bits of her scalp were raw and hairless. The whole time I was on my knees whimpering like a simpleton, she stroked my head with her good hand, telling me it was OK, that I shouldn't worry about a thing. She was twisting beneath the covers. I could feel the heat coming off her body. She was trying to smile at me, but her face wouldn't do what she wanted. "Just pray for me, Gilbert," she said. I tried—right there. I whispered a quick Our Father and a Hail Mary. I said an Act of Contrition. But the prayers got all mixed up in my mouth, and when I opened my eyes I was looking at a figurine of the Virgin Mary on a hospital tray next to the bed. Its face was calm. Its eyes were two small dabs of blue paint. I wanted to bite the head off that goddamn thing.

Every day after work I'd stop by the hospital with some fresh-baked bread, and she'd ask me to go back to Mass. I hadn't been to church since before my father died. I just shook my head. She knew what I was thinking—she was thinking the same damn thing. It was like this emptiness we shared. But she knew I'd never use it against her faith—not even later, when she was home and the burns started to itch.

Four old men in suits spread out and started working the pews, the silver poles of their collection baskets catching the light. The same guy who'd given me the bulletin came down our aisle, and the old lady and Johnny dropped some change into the felt basket. I pulled out the lining of my pocket. All I had was a fin. When I waved it, the guy slid the pole through the oilcloth mitt, and the basket rose up to meet my hand. I gave the lady with the kerchief a steady look. She went back to her rosary.

When Father Bluteau got to work on the host and the wine, everyone dropped to their knees, even Johnny. But there was no place for me to kneel on the stairs, not unless I faced away from the altar. So with my hands in my pockets I stood there—the only person on his feet in the church except the priest—and watched as he raised the big white wafer. A little bell rang. Now he was supposed to be holding up God in his hands for all to see. I wondered how many of the people kneeling between us believed it was so, how many thought they were clean enough to receive. Father Bluteau said, "Pray that our sacrifice may be acceptable to God, the Almighty Father." The kneelers murmured: "May the Lord accept the sacrifice at your hands for the praise and glory of His name, for our good, and the good of all His Church." They weren't machines this time. No. They sounded more like furniture being moved around on another floor of the building.

During Communion, I watched parishioners spill out of their pews into the center aisle. Johnny Dumas stayed on his knees. He looked like a nine-year-old kid. He was a better Catholic than me—he wouldn't even think of going up there drunk. My mother stood in the Communion line with her head down. From this distance, she looked like everyone else. But I knew her burns must still be oozing and itching beneath her clothes. She kept still. She took the host on her tongue and walked back to her pew, her head bent and her hands together. Only her lips would be moving. As I watched, something seemed to be breaking up inside me. I hadn't planned on receiving Communion, but then I thought, To hell with it. Why the hell not? I'm a little hungry anyways. I almost laughed out loud. If the fucker exists, I thought, he can take me as I am. I'm going up there. I stepped down the stairs, around Johnny, and I was walking fine. As I passed my mother and Aunt Yvonne's pew, I kept my head down and my hands together over my belt buckle — pure as the day of my First Communion.

When her skin had crusted up and flaked off like brown sugar, my mother came home from the hospital. The scars ran in bright red streaks from her chin, down across her left shoulder and breast, to the folds of her waist and her thighs. Aunt Yvonne came over to sit with her during the day while I worked, and the first week my mother slept well. It was going to be easy to take care of her, I thought. Just change her dressings before she went to sleep and in the morning, and hold her head while she took her medication. But by the second week she was up screaming three and four times a night. Before I was even awake, I'd be on my feet, my heart pounding in my ears. I'd stumble into her room, and she'd be lying there in sheets soaked through with blood, pus, and sweat. She'd be screaming about hell and sometimes calling out to my father. All I could think about was getting her to stop. I'd grab her by the shoulders and shake. Usually she'd calm down. Then I'd change her sheets and bandages and go back to bed.

One night, though, she wouldn't stop. She'd twisted over and over in her sleep until the bed covers had wrapped her legs together. Her eyes were open when I came into the room, but she seemed only half awake. "I can't stand it, Gil. I'm burning." It was like her voice wasn't hers anymore. I wet my hand with the glass of water and slapped her face — once, not too hard — but her screaming only got louder. "OK, Ma, it's all right," I said. "Here, take your Percocet." I fumbled with the lid. She pushed my hands away, and the bottle fell to the floor and rolled under the nightstand. I pulled her to me tight and hugged —

maybe I'd squeeze the pain out of her. She screamed in my ear. Then I started yelling myself. I punched the wall above the headboard. I tried shaking her again, so hard the bed scraped across the floor and the rosary beads rattled against the bedposts. She was wailing now. I stood back and looked at her thin arms there in the yellow light. Her hair was stuck to her forehead. She was so helpless. "Stop it, now, Ma," I said. She looked straight at me. "Now, Ma, please." My fist was numb and swelling. I closed it tight as I could. "Ma, stop it." Then I reached back, and, looking at the lampshade, I hit her with the back of my fist—once, twice, again, straight on, in the mouth, and finally she was quiet. She let her head fall to the pillow. A line of blood ran from her nose to her chin. I stood up. My face was wet. There, Ma, I thought. There's your God. He can let me do that to you. Her face seemed calmer now, but her eyes were like hot black rocks sinking into the snow. I fixed the bed sheets the way I did every night. Without a word, she rolled over so I could lay down a dry towel. I wiped her nose and her forehead with a damp facecloth. I left the light on, and she watched me as I backed out of the room. I was going to say something. But all I could feel was the heat in my fist. When I got into bed, I heard her voice again from the other room. She was saying the same thing over and over, but I couldn't hear exactly what it was. I covered my ears with my hands.

I was next in line to receive the Eucharist. When I stopped a little too close to Father Bluteau, he leaned back off balance. He must have caught a whiff of beer on me, because his leathery face tightened. He held the wafer away like he was shielding it from my breath. I stood there with my tongue out, a dog jumping for a snack. He shook his head just a little and waited for me to move on. I could see he was ripshit. When the woman behind me cleared her throat, I turned and walked off to the right—just as if I'd taken Communion—and kept walking out the side door.

In the cold night air again, I felt the stars on the back of my neck, the church rising behind me like a black wave. A priest shaking someone off in front of the altar, just flat out refusing someone the body of Christ—I'd never seen anything like it. I walked to the Mustang with my hands still crossed over my belt buckle.

When Johnny got in the car, he said, "Yeah, thanks for waiting for me."

"Guy refused to give me Communion," I said.

He laughed and put on his fedora. "You were drunk." He smoothed out the brim.

"Who the fuck is he to refuse me that?"

Johnny looked over at me like I was nuts. "He's a goddamn priest," he said. He started the car, put it in gear, and inched forward. The tire dropped off the curb with a scrape. "That's only his job, hose head," he said. "He's just taking care of business."

The bars along Acushnet Avenue were closed now. There was no one on the street. As we drove, a half-moon slipped behind the tenements and telephone poles. I tried to calm myself down. I cracked the window and let the air hit my face. Then I sank back into my seat, the plastic cold and brittle under my ass. But I couldn't get it out of my mind—Father Bluteau's face, all wrinkly and deflated. His wet eyes on me. Who the fuck did he think he was?

"I'm going back." I said, straightening up. "Let's go, now."

"Take it easy, Gil," Johnny said. "I mean, what's the big deal?" He reached back for a Narragansett. "Here," he said, handing me the can. "Narry Christmas."

All of a sudden I felt wicked panicky. "Turn around, Johnny."

"You haven't been to Mass in how long? Now you're bothered about this?"

"That son of a bitch is going to hear my confession." I couldn't go back to the apartment like that. Not tonight. I couldn't face my mother. "Going to church drunk is a sin."

"Right. And what about that little Maria you were feeling up earlier tonight?"

"That, too," I said. "Come on. Move it."

"I'm not turning around, Gil."

"You were drunk as me, Johnny. Just because you didn't go to Communion—you think God's going to split hairs? You were drunk in church." I snapped open the glove compartment, shoved the can of beer inside, and clicked the little door shut. "You and me, Johnny," I said. "Confession, now."

"No fucking way. It's like two in the morning."

"We both need it."

"Calm the fuck down, will you?"

I grabbed him by the back of the neck and squeezed. "Jesus," he yelled. He pushed me off. The car crossed into the oncoming lane, but it didn't matter. There was no one else on the road. He straightened out and kept driving.

"*Now*, Johnny." I slapped the back of his head. His hat fell off, and he locked up the brakes.

"You bastard," he said.

"Let me out here. I'll fucking walk."

"Goddamn it." He swung the car into a screeching three-point turn, and we drove back up the avenue to St. Anthony's. "You're one major-league pain in the ass, you know that?"

The church spotlights were out now, the spire black against the stars. I slid out of the car before we stopped and ran up the steps and inside. Empty like that, the place got my stomach churning even worse. I walked fast along the nave, the pews fanning by on either side of me. My footsteps echoed on the marble floor like they had that first day at the hospital on the way to my mother's room. When I saw Father Bluteau locking up the sacristy, I called out. He looked surprised to hear a voice, but he smiled. Just like a priest, I thought, ready for anything. He was wearing his full blacks. The gold vestments he'd worn at the Mass were tucked away somewhere now. He was new to the parish. I'd never met the man before that night. But my mother and Aunt Yvonne had talked about him often. They thought he was good-looking. He seemed smaller than he had standing on the altar, but he was well muscled in his shirtsleeves, trim for a guy in his early sixties. He stood there with his hands behind his back, smiling at me.

I said, "Father, I'm sorry." I was a little scared now.

When he saw who I was, his face fell. "I would hope so. Drunk on Christmas Eve. Drunk at Mass."

"Look, I know it was a dumb-ass thing to do."

His hands were working the air now. "Well, why don't you go home and think about it?" He turned to leave, but I grabbed his arm.

"I'm sorry."

"Me, too." His eyebrows way up, he shook himself free.

"Look, I'm sober now," I said. "Sober—" I stopped myself before I added, *as a nun*.

His face tightened, and he shoved his hands deep in his pockets. "This conversation is over."

"Father, you got to hear my confession." I was ready to tell all. Everything. I was thinking a priest should jump at such an offer. Wasn't that what they lived for?

"You're asking me to hear confession from a drunk man?"

"I told you. I'm sober."

He shook his head, just like the first time. I was that dog again, begging. Father Bluteau looked over my shoulder at Johnny. "He needs it, too," I said. The priest blew air through his lips. He turned and pushed his way through the door.

I couldn't let it go. I couldn't go back to the apartment like that. That son of a bitch was going to hear my confession. Johnny had me by the arm. "Gil, it's two o'clock in the morning," he said. I pushed him off and followed Father Bluteau outside. He was jogging across the parking lot to the rectory, his elbows pulled up tight to his body. His shoes flashed in the light from a street lamp.

When I called to him again, he shot me a half look over his shoulder and kept moving. "Goddamn it," I said. I ran down the steps and into the lot. Just as he turned, I grabbed him by the yoke of his black shirt. "Hey, I'm talking to you." His priest's collar snapped loose.

"Take your damn hands off me," he said, his voice lower now, almost a growl. I wanted to let him go. I tried. But it was like my hands didn't belong to me anymore, and the only way to get them back was to keep them right where they were. I heard Johnny behind me. He slipped his arm around my neck —a loose half nelson. I knew he didn't want to hurt me. I shot an elbow into his gut, and he fell back, gasping.

"Listen," I said, tightening my grip on Father Bluteau's shirt. His face was red. He was breathing heavily. But I felt calmer now. If God had watched my mother burn, if He had watched me beat her, He was watching now, and I wasn't afraid. Fuck no. I was here to get what was mine. "I'm not leaving till you hear my confession," I said. "You're going to hear me out."

He kept his eyes on mine. He didn't blink. "And I'm telling you I'm not giving absolution to anyone who comes into my church drunk. It wouldn't mean a damn thing if I did. Now, you go home, and you get to bed." He leaned back, pulling me off balance. He grabbed my wrists and twisted, but I held him tight.

"Please—" I said. His knee snapped up into my balls, and I crumpled to the tar.

I couldn't believe it.

I was squirming, trying to shuck off the pain. "Father," I said. "You son of a bitch." He tried to help me up, but I'd locked my hands around my knees. I wasn't going anywhere. I watched his black shoes step over me. He apologized. His voice seemed to come from somewhere far above. He said something to Johnny. Then he walked off toward the rectory.

Serves you right, asshole," Johnny said on the way back to my place. "Who do you think you are? Grabbing a priest like that." The pain in my balls had spread upward like hot black ink into my stomach. I was slumped in my seat, cupping my crotch with both hands. Whenever the car hit a pothole, the pain flared up, and my forehead thudded against the cold window. Two blocks ahead, a prostitute crossed the street on wobbly heels. The lamps of the interstate overpass shed a pale orange light down onto Route 18. There was no one else in sight. "I ought to make you walk," Johnny said. But then he shut up, and it didn't take long before I could tell he was feeling sorry for me. I hadn't elbowed him that hard. He'd forgiven me. Johnny was a good Catholic.

When we pulled up to the curb in front of my tenement, he pushed back his hat and slapped my shoulder. "Don't worry about it, Gil. There's like four masses you can go to tomorrow." I opened the door, climbed out of the car, and tried to stand up straight in the cold night air. Above me, the apartment windows were lit. "You need some help?" he asked, stifling a smile.

"No, thanks," I said. "But fuck-thee-well, anyway."

Johnny laughed.

I waved him off and slammed the car door. Then I turned and hobbled across the sidewalk to the front entrance of the tenement. But after Johnny tore off down the street, I went back to the curb and watched the Mustang's taillights until they disappeared.

I took my time climbing the stairs to the apartment. We lived on the third floor, and I had to rest on the dark landings with my hands on my knees. When I opened the door, Aunt Yvonne stood up from the couch with a cigarette in her hand. She motioned me to be quiet. "Your mother's asleep," she whispered. She took one last pull on the cigarette and crunched out the butt in the ceramic fish ashtray I'd made in junior high. Aunt Yvonne was a large woman, six years older than my mother. Besides being sisters, they had other things in common. Aunt Yvonne's husband had died a decade before, and her two kids lived far away. I hadn't seen them in years. For a while after the night I hit my mother, I worried Aunt Yvonne might find out. But when nothing changed, I knew that it was between my mother and me, and that it would always be this way.

I took off my jacket and shoes and limped to the refrigerator for a beer. "How was Mass?" I said over my shoulder. My mother had said something once about praying in a closet, and it seemed to make sense to me now. It would be our little secret —another one. Some gifts are personal, no matter how fucked up. When I turned around, Aunt Yvonne was standing there with her hands on her bulky hips, slowly shaking her head. "You want a beer?" I asked.

"Christmas Eve." Now she was nodding, but I could tell she didn't want one. "It was the least you could do, Gilbert." She zipped up her coat on the way to the door.

"I know." I really didn't want her to leave. I held up two cans. "We got Schlitz and we got Budweiser."

She rattled her car keys. "Your mother doesn't ask much of you."

"I know, Aunt Yvonne." I cracked open the beer.

After she left, I walked around the apartment, snapping off lamps one at a time. This year my mother had put the crèche on the kitchen table where the bowl of wax fruit usually was. We never ate there anyway. The manger was this small house without walls. It was made from gray particleboard, the corners chipped and splintered. As a kid, I'd stuck bits of cotton to the roof for snow. When it was dark, the figures lit up automatically.

I sat down on the couch in what me and my mother called the living room. I left the television screen black and sipped my beer and listened to her uneven breathing coming from the other room. I sat there that way for a long time, thinking about waking her up. It was already Christmas Day.

Welcome Wagon

RED OWNED a unit in the Blue Pines Mobile Village. Kitchen in the corner, dining room almost twice as wide as he was tall, toilet and shower, waterbed at the far end. He parked his GTO under the corrugated green fiberglass roof of the carport he'd built years earlier.

One night around dusk he woke up and dressed and went out on the small wooden deck to smoke a joint. It wasn't dark yet, even though the sun was gone. Down the street, he heard the loud voices of the Smayle brothers and their biker friends. Sometimes the air boiled with the noise of their mufflerless motorcycles. Dishes rattled in the cupboards. Dogs, cats, and mice ran for the trees. Some nights Red imagined the worms shrinking away, digging deeper into their moist tunnels. He'd tried to talk to the Smayles about it, but they told him to go fuck off. They were crazy sons of bitches. Jimmy Smayle bit open bottles of beer. Jack pulled his own teeth with vise grips. They gave each other tattoos. Red could deal with the noise.

He decided to fire up the hibachi. He stepped into the trailer, snapped on the deck light, and came back outside with an aluminum chair, a package of linguiça, and a bottle of Rolling Rock. He lit the grill and sat down to drink the beer. He'd jammed his middle finger in a fight at work that day. As the charcoal reddened and crumpled, he pulled at the dirty medical tape around the metal splint with his teeth.

There was a new woman in the park. Two trailers down and across the lane. Unit number three. He could see the light from her kitchen. Every once in a while, her head cast a shadow on the window. She was divorced. He knew this because he'd lain awake one Saturday night with the windows open, listening to her chat with Mrs. Souza. She had to be about forty, with long dark hair. Sort of Hispanic-looking. A little on the hefty side. She had a couple of kids, but he'd only seen them once. The night she moved in, as she drank from the unit's garden hose, he'd given her one of his little waves, and she'd smiled. That was about a week ago. Leticia. He'd never known anyone with that name.

Red turned the linguiça over with a pair of crusty lettuce tongs. The meat was curling up. He had an idea. Jesus, why not take a plate over for this Leticia woman? What would she say? His little contribution to the Welcome Wagon. He laid another open roll facedown on the grill and looked over at Leticia's kitchen window again. A spider plant hung in a macramé holder. He'd get out that wooden tray with the handles and fix up two plates with chips and yellow mustard and a couple of open beers. Why the fuck not? If she wanted, he'd roll a bone or two.

As the linguiça finished cooking, he went in and put on the cleanest jeans he could find. He retaped the splint. He sniffed out a clean white T-shirt and shook out his blazer. Then he soaped up his face and head and rinsed off.

Five minutes later, he was crossing the lane to number three. The clouds had broken. A few stars hovered over the pine trees. Balancing the tray on his knee, he knocked. Leticia leaned out a window. "Yes?" She was smiling politely.

"Ah, yeah. I'm Red. I live a few units down?"

"Who?"

He jerked his head in the direction of his trailer. "Red."

"Do I know you?"

"Well, no," he said, "but—"

"Let me come around."

Red waited. He heard one of the Smayle brothers screaming down the lane. A motorcycle began to rumble, then fell silent. "What the hell am I doing?" he said under his breath.

She opened the door. She wore a sweatshirt over jeans and red high-top sneakers. She was chunkier than he remembered. But her face was pretty. She had great eyes, which were looking at him with confusion, her eyebrows all bunched up.

"Leticia, right?"

"Yeah."

Red held up the tray. Years before, he'd burnt the Boston Bruins logo in the center of it with a soldering iron. "Have you eaten?"

She looked at her watch. "Yes, I have."

"I just thought I'd bring a little something over. I was cooking up some linguiça on the grill back there. I wondered if you were hungry. You like linguiça, or what?"

"Who are you again?"

"Red."

"Gee." She looked over her shoulder. "I'm on my way out, Red."

"Hey, no problem."

"If you want to come in for a sec." She held the door as he brushed past, feeling the warmth of her arm against his. The kitchen was done up in some kind of rustic style. Rooster stencils along the tops of the walls, pairs of candles hanging on nails from uncut wicks. Red hated that shit. He put the tray down on the table.

"Can I leave you a plate?"

"What is it again?" She still had her hand on the door.

"Red."

"No. The food."

"That there's linguiça. A linguiça sandwich. I got you some mustard there, too." He'd stuck a butter knife in a jar of French's. He felt like an idiot pointing at the tray. "There's a Rolling Rock beer there."

"Thanks, Red. I'm late. I got to drive."

Red started nodding. "Yeah, I got to go to work in a little while anyway." Fuck it, he thought. What an asshole I am. What a prime-time asshole.

"You think it will keep?"

"Linguiça? Oh, sure."

"I'll put it in the refrigerator for later."

"No problem."

She looked at the beer. "I really don't drink. Sorry."

"Oh, OK," he said. "I'll take them with me."

"Thanks, though." She opened the door a little wider. "You caught me at a bad time."

"Like I said. No problem." He picked up the tray and squeezed past her again. He walked back across the rutted lane and sat down on the deck. He drank the beers and ate the sandwich, waiting for Leticia to leave. But it was an hour before the lights went dark in the window and she came out and got into her car and drove away. "Fuck me," Red said. He pinched out his roach and went back into the trailer to get ready for work.

Bakery

THE FIRST TIME he saw Red, Gus was leaning against the cooling ovens with some of the other men from his shift, drinking coffee and staring out the six-foot windows of the bakery's third floor. The morning sun squatted on the Fairhaven side of the Acushnet River like a flattened neon ball. Gus had spent sixteen hours feeding cast-iron trays to an antique dough-press machine. His wrists and elbows ached. His lungs were raw. He was still new at the Our Bread Baking Company, still on call, and the night foreman used him wherever and whenever he was needed, sometimes filling in for guys who were sick, sometimes spelling workers during their breaks.

Suddenly, someone was hooting and laughing behind him, the noise getting louder as it echoed in the long room. When he turned, he saw a short, heavy guy with a flattop and a weedy red beard marching toward him and the other men. "I got bird duty," the man bellowed. "Make fucking way, gentlemen." Gus stepped aside. The man threw open one of the windows and bent over, the crack of his ass showing above the waistband of his dirty work whites. He started laying bread dough on the stone ledge. "Come and get it," he yelled. Gus moved forward for a better look. Pigeons had already begun gathering, grunting and slapping their wings in the damp morning air, clawing at the granite. "Eat up," the man said. The beaks darted forward again and again. "That's right, you dumb motherfuckers." Two gooey dabs of flour dust clung to the corners of his mouth.

Who is this clown? thought Gus. One of his co-workers leaned forward and whispered, "Have you met Red yet?"

Gus shook his head.

"You don't know what you're missing."

Gus finished his coffee in one final swig. He was trying to look unimpressed, but the sound of Red's high-pitched voice and the sight of his red-rimmed eyes had sent something scurrying inside him.

"He does this every day," said the co-worker. "Oh, and check this out—Red's next in line to be foreman, in a month or so, when Claude retires."

Gus shrugged. He told himself not to say a word. What did he care? Red hadn't noticed him. Gus didn't want any problems. He was smart enough to know how stray comments could get around. He couldn't afford to lose another job. He told himself to keep out of Red's way, just ignore him.

With his head outside in the high morning air, Red felt the sunlight on his cheeks as he watched the pigeons peck and turn, peck and turn their heads, their necks color-shifting from black to green and back again. He loved to see them gobble up the warm dough, loved it when they launched into the air and spun thirty-five feet to the sidewalk. When the dough expanded in their stomachs, the birds couldn't fly. It had to do with wing-to-volume ratio—he had it all figured out. "Look at them," he said under his breath. He stood up and cocked his head, snickering as he waited for the pop on the pavement below. "Not the smartest creatures I've ever seen," he said aloud. "Well, fuck 'em."

His sharp-cornered flattop neatly waxed, Red had always thought of himself as a somewhat shorter, somewhat boxier version of Johnny Unitas. Under his white apron, he wore a rose-colored T-shirt. He refused to wear a hardhat, but because he'd worked twenty years at the bakery, no one said a word. At least not to his face. His real name was Gilbert. He was French Canadian, and when he was fourteen some punks had heard his mother call him "Jeel"—short for "Jeel-bear"—and he'd never heard the end of it. He renamed himself. He preferred Red.

In the weeks to come, whenever the pace let up and the conveyor belts scraped to a stop, Gus saw Red wander over from the hamburger roll machine to where Prak, the Cambodian kid, was sweeping or pushing a dolly of bread trays. Red gave Prak and his brother a lot of shit. No one knew why. At first it was nothing serious. Red would tap Prak on the shoulder, then duck around the other side. "What the fuck kind of name is Prak?" He'd knock the kid's hardhat to the floor and crouch into a boxer's stance. Then he'd bob and weave, his beard net flapping like a dirty scrotum against the fat folds in his neck. "Raging Bull, I'm telling you. Raging Fucking Bull. You heard of LaMotta? I'll jelly your head, son. You don't want to tangle with me." Gary, the other guy on Red's machine, stood back, laughing.

During break one time, Red told the Cambodian he needed a new name. "Prak's bullshit," he said. "You're in America now. You're Bert now." Some of the guys in the break room spilled coffee all over themselves, tears in their eyes. Others were less entertained. Gus was glad of this—he didn't want to stand out. As for Prak, he smiled thinly. Like Gus, he was new at the bakery. From that day forward Red gave Prak new names. Howard, Zeke, Gunther. One night, over the intercom, a voice paged someone named Billy Bob up to the main office. It took a minute, but then everyone knew which person Red must have been talking about. More often than not, though, Prak was Bert.

Prak couldn't have been older than seventeen or eighteen, a

quiet guy with narrow shoulders and long, thin fingers, his nails neatly filed and clean. The visor of the white hardhat they'd given him rode low over his eyes. Whenever Gus saw him, he thought of a war documentary he'd seen on cable: a long line of soldiers with red towels tied to their heads sneaking single file through a tropical forest. Prak's older brother, Lok, made croutons in a room on the third floor. Gus had done it himself, and it was far from fun breathing in that crumb dust above the whine of the grinder. Neither Prak nor Lok spoke much English. They kept to themselves. But one time Lok sat down next to Gus during the long break, pointed to an advertisement for Camaros in the newspaper Gus was reading, and smiled. He tried to form the word. Gus grinned back and said it slowly, loudly, the way he'd heard people talk to foreigners and deaf people. "Ca-ma-ro." Lok nodded and offered Gus a little boiled pork from a crumple of tin foil. But Gus shook his head no and held up his baloney sandwich. One of the guys who worked the big ovens sat across the room with his feet up on the windowsill. He'd been looking out at the traffic, listening to their conversation. Paste-white scars covered his forearms where he'd burned himself on the heavy baking trays. Without turning his head, he hawked and spat on the floor between his legs and mumbled something that Gus pretended not to hear. Lok pretended, too. But for the rest of the break they ate in silence, and Gus started thinking about how in hell this Cambodian guy and his younger brother had ended up here, in New Bedford, Massachusetts.

If Gus didn't like the Our Bread Baking Company, it was his own fault he'd ended up there. He'd had it good. When his father couldn't work anymore, Gus had bought the house-painting business from him. He took out another loan and bought a black Dodge utility van with tan carpeting in the cab and a roof rack for the forty-foot aluminum ladder and the scaffolding pipes. He had two magnetic signs made up and slapped them on the front doors: LAPOINT PROFESSIONAL PAINTERS. GUS LAPOINT, JR., PROPRIETOR. INTERIORS, EXTERIORS. WALL-PAPERING. They were doing all right, Gus and his wife, Pam. They'd moved into a large apartment. It was above a funeral home, but it was roomier than anything they'd been able to afford up to that time. They were trying to save for a house. They even thought about having kids. Pam had gone back to school at the local community college.

It had been hard painting alone, but his father had thrown in Homer with the deal. Homer was an epileptic who'd overdosed on an experimental drug back in 1946. He knew how to mix paint and hold the foot of the ladder while someone scraped an eave; he'd walk around with a pencil behind his ear. Every time Gus's father had offered to pay him, Homer backed away with his hands in his armpits. Homer couldn't do any heavy lifting anymore, but Gus didn't mind having him around. He didn't talk too much, didn't fill Gus's ear with nonsense. He was like a quiet uncle.

One Sunday morning in December, Gus and Homer were driving out to a high school gymnasium to drop off some tarps and scaffolding for a big interior job the next day. Gus had gone barhopping with his Vermont cousin Pierre the night before. Pam had been at her business ethics class over at Bristol Community College, so he hadn't seen any reason not to let loose a little. That morning he was trying to stretch what was left of his buzz past noon.

On Route 6, just beyond the Mattapoisett Diner, Gus fiddled with the radio, an open beer cooling the insides of his thighs. Homer had his own can, but he wasn't drinking it. He liked to warm it up in his hands first. Just as Gus zeroed in on one of his favorite Led Zeppelin tunes, Homer let out a horrendous howl and pounded the dashboard with both fists. He'd seen the Monte Carlo stopped in the left lane, its directionals flashing. Gus locked the brakes and threw out his right arm to keep Homer's head from dome-denting the windshield. The road was still white with night frost, and the van drifted into a creeping spin, sliding past the median and coming to rest sideways across the two westbound lanes. The rosary beads Gus's mother had given him rocked against the stem of the rearview mirror, the little silver cross dancing. He looked over at Homer. "Are you all right?" Just then something slammed into the double side doors, ripping the rolls of tarpaulin off the roof rack. The scaffolding pipes rang all around them like cathedral bells.

Homer whimpered above the static of the radio. "It's all right," Gus said. He rolled the beer can under his seat and got out of the van. A light mist was falling. Under a nest of pipes, a yellow Volvo station wagon lay on its side, the driver's window streaked with blood. "Oh, Christ," Gus whispered. His breath hung in a cloud. "Jesus H. Christ." But as he edged closer to the car, the fist around his lungs seemed to unclench. The blood was paint. Cans of latex were rolling down the highway. The driver of the Volvo sent up a wail, calling out for someone named Amanda. Then the two kids in the back seat started bawling.

Cars slowed to pass single file between the wreck and the curb. The drivers stared at Gus, some of them wide-eyed and scared, some pissed off, their mouths working behind the glass. He wanted to pound their windshields: What are you looking at? But then the nervousness was draining out of him. He'd been driving without a license or insurance. He wasn't yet thinking of what he'd tell Pam. He was thinking about one last swig of beer. He had a feeling it would be his last for a while.

Gus had been on call a month before the bakery slotted him on regular third shift: 11:00 P.M. to 7:00 A.M. He felt damn lucky to get the steady work. They put him on a machine that sliced and bagged hot dog rolls—part of a two-man crew—with a guy named Frank, who was six foot six and didn't have a hair on his shiny head.

The hot dog rolls bumped along on a conveyor belt that started at the mouth of an oven on the second floor, wound through the girders and support beams, and passed in front of Gus as he sat on a stool half his height. His job was simple — make sure the rolls didn't jam the slicer. "You got to regulate the flow of buns," Frank said. "They got to go in straight." Frank's huge hands moved quickly over the belt, shuffling the yellow bread as it tumbled past, flicking away a torn roll. "And keep your mitts out of the slicer."

Gus nodded.

"That's a sharp motherfucker," Frank said. He held up the ragged end of a spindled piece of cardboard he'd shoved into the machine.

"Sure is," Gus said. The image of Pam's smooth thigh flashed into his mind.

"You don't believe me?"

"I believe you."

At six o'clock, the morning light from the bakery's high windows shot beams through the drifting flour. Across the floor, Red and Gary had finished early — no more bulky rolls to be bagged. Gary was pulling apart their machine, while Red leaned against the wall with a can of soda. Red was thinking about bird duty. Maybe there'd be some mourning doves. Maybe he'd grab one of those fucking pigeons and bring it home with him, build a coop. He was waiting for someone to show up with a compression cleaner and start blasting dust and bread bits out of the guts of the rig.

When Red saw Prak, he rapped Gary on the hardhat with his knuckles. "Shit," Gus said below the rumble of the machine. He knew what was coming. He wanted to say something to Frank, but he didn't want to come off like a pussy. It was his first regular night, for God's sake. Prak could take care of himself. But he felt guilty because even though he'd started at the bakery after Prak, he'd already come off call.

Prak attached the nozzle of the compression cleaner to one of the blue hoses that hung from the ceiling. He ignored Red. His movements were quick and precise. Adjusting his hardhat, the Cambodian tested the connection twice — two short bursts of air that echoed across the bakery's cement floor. Then he walked to the far end of the machine and got to work. A thick cloud of flour rose around him.

Red gave a sharp whistle. Gary stopped what he was doing and stood up. He was about Gus's age, twenty-eight, a wiry guy with a long neck that seemed attached to his shoulders at a forty-five-degree angle. Gus could see his Adam's apple toggling up and down as he talked. Red held the soda can at arm's length and crushed it in his fist. Bending his knees, he paused as though aiming a basketball, then arced the can into the air. It bounced off Prak's hardhat and spun away with a clatter. Prak kept working. Red walked over and leaned on the hood of his machine's slicer. He crossed his glossy blue boots at the ankle. He had all the time in world.

Gus tapped Frank's tattooed arm.

"What?" Frank's face was creased with flour. "Red? The guy's an asshole. What do you want me to do about it?" He went back to stacking and turning the rolls as they came out of the slicer.

"Shouldn't we say something to Claude?" Claude, the night foreman who was scheduled to retire, spent most of his time with a cigar in the second-floor office.

"Huh?" Frank bunched his face up on one side. "Leave it alone. What do you care?"

Red picked up a push broom and began to play it like a guitar, his fingers sliding up and down the handle. Mississippi Delta blues—he loved them. He was Muddy Waters. He was Elmore James. Gary shook his head, grinning, his arms crossed. "You're nuts," he said. Red turned the broom around and diddled the end of it in Prak's ribs. The kid kept reaching in among the belts and gears, blowing flour and bits of debris out onto the floor.

Then Red bopped Prak's helmet with the end of the handle, not hard, a firm tap. It reminded Gus of how you might go about knighting someone with a sword. He did it again, harder this time, and the hiss of the compression cleaner suddenly stopped. Prak rose from his crouch. Red looked around, smiling, his eyes pink and wide. He threw the broom down and spanked his fat chest with his fists. He'd flatten the kid right there. No questions asked. Gus could hear him now: "Come on. I got your number, Bert. I got your fucking number."

Gary hooted and started clapping.

"Frank, what is this?" Gus said. Frank ignored him. "What the hell?" But Gus didn't move. Hot dog rolls were piling up at the mouth of the slicer.

Red inched closer to Prak until they stood a foot apart. He outweighed the kid by at least a hundred pounds. Prak pushed back his hardhat. He was thin and fragile as a breadstick next to Red. When Red gave him a quick shove with the tips of his fingers, Prak held his ground. His face was stony now, his hands low at his side but tense. He was ready for action. Red shoved him again, and this time Prak raised the nozzle of the hose and blasted Red in the face with a burst of compressed air. Gus almost fell off his stool. "Motherfucker," Red said softly. He stood perfectly still for a second, his cheeks full and pink. "Well, I'll be fucked and fried." He lunged for the Cambodian, and they tumbled back into a column of stainless steel bread trays, which, teetering for a second, crashed to the floor with a huge racket. Then a crowd of helmets surrounded the two. In his green foreman's hat, Claude stood between them with a hand on each of their chests as the men held them back. Red was laughing about how he'd been teaching Prak to dance. "The kid's got two left feet. What can I say?" He started hacking. "Sorry about those trays, Claude." Prak's eyes shot wildly back and forth, his wet face straining in the sunlight. Gus thought he must have been looking for Lok.

A few minutes later, Red and Gary walked past Gus's machine. Gus kept his head down, his eyes on the belt. It was almost time to punch out. Red's blue boots stopped a few feet away. He was waiting for Gus to look up, but Gus kept working. "You got a fucking problem?" Red said, his voice rough and phlegmy. When Gus raised his eyes, Red shoved his pudgy face out in front of him. Flour had settled into the wax of his flattop.

He was still breathing heavily. He looked like a fat angel in a church painting, an angel with a serious attitude.

Gus shook his head mutely.

"You sure, pal?" Red had his hands on his wide hips. "Because, you know, I'm like a handyman around here. You got a problem, I can fix it, *tout de suite*." Gary laughed. Red stood like that till Gus looked down at the belt again. Then he turned to walk away.

"What if I do?" Gus said. The words jumped out of him. He felt his heart now. He'd never been much of a brawler.

Red came back to the belt. "What was that?"

Gus shook his head again.

"No, what did you just say?"

"Shit," said Frank. "Give me a break."

"You asked me if I had a problem," Gus said slowly. "And I answered with a question: 'What if I do?'"

"And I said I could fix your problem." Red's eyes were glassy, bloodshot. He was smiling and scowling, both. He was hungry, hungry for rough words. It was like a burning.

"I don't think I like the shit you're giving Prak."

"You mean Bert?" Red said.

"I think his name's Prak." The buns wouldn't stop coming long enough for Gus to look Red in the eyes.

"Jesus Christ, Red, take a walk," Frank said. "We're trying to finish up here."

"Hey, Frank." Red flicked a hand in his direction. "Fuck you, if you don't mind. We're trying to clear something up here. Is that all right with you? Do I have your permission? We got us an honest difference of opinion." But then, suddenly, it was over. Frank went back to his stacking, and Red turned to Gary and said, "Come on, pencil neck. Time to feed the birds." They walked away.

There's this guy at work," Gus said to Pam. It was 8:30. They'd just gotten through with their morning quickie. Up until the day Gus wrecked the van and lost the business, they hadn't been using anything. They hadn't worried about it. They told themselves they'd leave it to chance. "Come what may," Pam had joked. It was nice. But they'd had to put the brakes on that. Nothing seemed certain anymore. That morning Gus was happy to climb back into the cool sheets with Pam. But while he was moving up into her, all he could see was the flour dust in Red's flattop. Pam came in a quick sharp rush, but Gus just couldn't make it over the hill himself, his cock feeling heavy and dead inside the condom as he pulled out. Now he sat in his bathrobe at the kitchen table, eating a bowl of Frosted Mini-Wheats with a New York State collector's spoon and looking out at the tops of the houses and the river while Pam got ready for work in the bathroom. "His name's Red."

"What?"

"A guy at work," Gus said.

"I heard that. What about him?"

"He's been leaning on this other new guy."

"Leaning? You sound like such a tough guy since you're working at the bakery. I love it." Pam walked out into the kitchen in her Friendly's uniform—a white blouse under a brown polyester outfit with white pinstripes, vest, pants, and an apron with a nametag that read, "Hello. I'm Pam. Ask me about the new Double Fribble." They made her wear a plastic visor, but she didn't put it on until she got there. She stood half an inch taller than Gus, a thin woman with long gangly limbs, hair the color of coffee and cream, and a habit of bunching her chin into her neck, doubling and even tripling the skin under her jaw. Her face and body were widely freckled. After Gus wrecked the van, she'd had to go back to her job—no more courses at the community college. She wasn't pleased. She hadn't settled on a major yet; it had been a toss-up between hotel management with a minor in nineteenth-century philosophy or vice versa. "Why's he leaning on him?"

"I don't really know. He's foreign."

"Who? Red?"

"No. This new guy." Gus didn't tell her how new Prak was. "What's his name?"

"Prak."

"Yeah? What kind of a name is that?"

"That's what Red was asking. It's Cambodian. But Red renamed him."

"Renamed him? What did he rename him?"

"Bert."

Pam laughed. She put her hand over her mouth and bunched her chin. Gus looked at her without smiling.

"I'm sorry," she said. "That's unkind. But it is funny."

"Not for Prak, it isn't." Gus scraped milk from his chin stubble with the spoon. "I don't know about this guy Red, though." But as soon as he said it, he knew what Pam was thinking. It was his tone of voice. She didn't want to hear any bitching about the job. He could tell by her look. As a waitress at Friendly's she had to deal with elderly people who sent back a $3.50 hamburger two or three times. "It says 'golden brown' in the menu," they'd say. "I'd like it golden brown." Little kids threw up their milk shakes in the booths almost every morning. The manager made her mop the floors three times a day and clean both toilets twice a week. How long would Gus last at that job? she had asked him. He could put up with a little bullshit from some guy named Red.

She stepped into her shoes. "Can't Prak take care of himself?" Gus was past trying to explain some things to her. She had a way of moving the discussion right by him before what he wanted to say could fully form in his mouth. Some things took time to say. It had been like that when he'd tried to tell her about the accident, and the way the van and the Volvo seemed to rotate like a single thing while he sat on the curb and told himself it didn't matter. She wouldn't hear it. "We're in debt up to our asses," she'd yelled. It was too late to get their money back from the college. "Now I have to go back to work in the fucking mall? It does matter, Gus. It matters to me." But that's not what he'd meant, not exactly. It all depended on how far you could stand back from such a thing. You needed distance. She just couldn't stand back as far as he could.

When Pam left for work, Gus carried what was left of his

bowl of cereal into the den. He snapped on the television and fell back into the couch. He knew he should be trying to sleep, but he kept seeing Red. The more he thought about him, the worse he wanted a bottle of Labatt's, maybe two or three. Mornings had always been the worst time. Some days, he'd get this heavy feeling that seemed to start in his balls and move up inside, as though he were being filled with cement. The only thing that could melt it out of him was a six-pack. That's how he'd lost his license. He'd never been a steady drinker. He'd binge for a day or two, then be sober for months.

Gus watched some of the morning shows, Kathie Lee and the cheery asshole that sat next to her. He flipped past Geraldo and Donahue. Jerry Springer had guests who wanted to marry their own uncles. He lingered on one of the fitness programs. A dozen people were doing knee pushups in front of a parrot. The women looked nice in their tight workout gear. Gus fingered his pecker a little through the slot in his boxers. It firmed up again, and he tugged his balls free of his thighs. He spat on his palm, but it was no use. The parrot's neck was the same color as Red's glossy boots. That morning they'd been dusted with a thin layer of flour, and as Gus sat there with his penis in his palm like a sticky fish, all he could think about was wiping those boots clean. "You got a fucking problem?" he heard Red say. Gus tried to laugh, but the sound came out more like a one-syllable sob.

Finally, he turned off the television and got back into bed. He tried a few deep-breathing exercises. These seemed to help. He was finally settling down. He looked over at the green numbers of the clock. He'd be back at the bakery in fifteen hours. He listened to the traffic out on the street. It had rained, and the tires of the cars hissed as they passed. The sound became a whisper as he drifted in and out of consciousness. He heard the voice of Mr. Medeiros, the funeral director, coming from the parking lot just before he fell asleep.

But then he was sitting up in bed, a horrendous banging competing with the pulse in his neck. Sometimes he and Pam would hear distant wailing—Portuguese wakes with elderly mourners in the funeral home two floors below. But these noises were distinctly inhuman thuds coming from above. Gus stood up and put his robe back on. He walked from one end of the apartment to the other, trying to zero in on the source. He opened one of the windows and leaned out, the cold air in his nostrils, but he couldn't see anything. Then he put Pam's furry slippers on and stamped down the two flights of stairs and out into the parking lot. He saw a black Dumpster that hadn't been there when he'd come home, and a pickup truck with a utility cabinet in the back bed. Oh, shit, he thought. A ladder climbed the side of the building. Big chunks of tarpaper were leafing through the air. He had to step out of the way to avoid being hit.

"Hey," he called up. It was cold and drizzling. "Hey, what the hell's up, up there?" A head in a black knit cap leaned over the edge of the building. "What's going on?" The man raised his chin sharply.

"Roofers," he said.

"What? You got to be kidding me." Gus threw his hands up and looked around. "I got to sleep." The man's head disappeared for a minute, then came back with another head.

"What's the problem?" said the second man. He had this smart-ass grin.

"I work at night," Gus yelled. "I can't have this. I sleep in the day."

"Talk to the landlord." He pointed downward. "We're putting in a new roof."

"How long's it going to take?"

"Two weeks—tops."

"Oh, shit." Gus was standing in the middle of the lot in a pair of women's slippers. He looked across the street at the R & P Tavern. It hadn't opened for business yet.

"Talk to the landlord. Sorry, man. Talk to Mr. Medeiros."

He walked around the building and pushed through the front door. That was where the funeral home received the grieving. There was a short vestibule with an oak lectern and a small white book for guest signings. The place smelled like air freshener. The pounding and tearing had begun again. He walked through a room set up with chairs and a raised platform for a casket. "Hey, Mr. Medeiros?" he called. No one answered. Just after the accident, Gus and Homer had painted the south side of the building in exchange for three months' rent. But Gus had never been inside the funeral home. He followed a carpeted hallway, opening doors as he went—a closet, a toilet, an empty room with the shades drawn, narrow stairs going down to the basement. "Hey, Mr. Medeiros?" A door marked "Private" opened, and, putting on the jacket of his gray suit, Mr. Medeiros stepped out.

"Yes?" he said. "Hello, Gus." Mr. Medeiros was about ten years older than Gus, a tall, thin, washed-out guy, just the man you'd want to have run a funeral—if you'd never heard what he said when he thought no one was listening. When Gus and Pam first moved in, sometimes Gus would press his ear to the radiator pipe in the bathroom and listen to the conversation of the morticians and their helpers two floors below. One time he heard them talking about the shape of a dead guy's penis, how it wouldn't go down, no matter what. He hadn't been able to sleep all night.

"Mr. Medeiros, I don't want to be a pain in the ass," he said, "but I'm working nights now. I'm sleeping days. I can't have this kind of banging up there."

"Gee, Gus." Mr. Medeiros had a good voice for funerals and wakes, soft and deep and always disappointed. "I don't know what we're going to do here." He didn't let himself notice Gus's slippers.

"Like I said, I don't want to be a pain in the ass, but I got to work. You know what I'm talking about?"

"Sure, Gus, I know. The problem is, I've already contracted with these fellows." He crossed his arms and cupped his chin in his hand. "It'll only be for a week or two."

Gus looked over his shoulder into the room Mr. Medeiros had come out of. He saw what he thought was the bare foot of a dead guy. It was long, and white as a tooth.

"I'd offer you one of the rooms down here." Mr. Medeiros smiled thinly. "What's your schedule like?"

"Down here?" Gus said. "No, that's all right. I'll deal with it." He thanked Mr. Medeiros for the offer.

That night, Red kept calling guys over as though he needed help, then holding up his hand, the white medical tape fluttering loose from the splint that held his middle finger rigid. He'd jammed the finger in the scuffle with Prak. "Oh, man," he said, "I'm awfully sorry." Gary laughed again and again. Most of the other guys weren't amused beyond a snort. When Red tried it on Claude, Claude told him to grow the fuck up. Every once in a while Red would look across the room at Gus. He would jab a finger in his direction and smile, then suddenly get all mean and serious in the face. "Jesus Christ," Frank said. "That guy's going to be foreman soon." Gus didn't say anything. He kept his head down, his hands working the rolls. Now and then Red yodeled at the ceiling: "Bert!" Prak was nowhere around.

At about two in the morning, during a short letup in the stream of hot dog rolls, there was a noise in the next room that sounded like a truck slamming into the side of the bakery. Even Frank seemed surprised. Gus heard laughing, shouts. Then someone screamed and started moaning. When they ran into the room, one of the dough-press men lay on the floor with his foot under an enormous blob of bread dough, fresh cracks in the wooden flooring all around it. "Oh, shit," he kept saying. "No, I'm all right, really." Upstairs, a small crew mixed the dough in ten-foot-long steel chutes that tilted up on one end with a hydraulic pump. The dough slid out of the oiled trough, flopping down like a fat whale through a hatch directly above the funnel of the dough press. The funnel squeezed the dough into tubes and shat it out in five-inch-long segments for the rising ovens. "I forgot to swing the funnel over," the dough-press man said. "It's all my fault." He had tears in his eyes.

When Claude saw what had happened, he was hot. "Oh, my fucking word," he said. He pointed up through the hatch at some of the faces looking at him. "Down here, now." Then he started grabbing at everyone he could, pulling them off balance, shoving them ahead of him. He bawled out the man under the dough blob. "I want everyone in the break room, now, now, now." His face was red-streaked and pimpled with sweat. "This shift is shitting the bed big time. Let's go."

The break room had been a retail thrift shop for the bakery. It was barely big enough for the thirty guys working that night. Gus squeezed in against the wall with Frank and some of the oven men, while Claude walked back and forth on a bench he'd pulled up close to what had once been display windows. The room's lights shone in the glass behind him. Claude was a thin Canuck with short, stubby legs, the cuffs of his work pants always folded halfway to his knees. Black hair showed beneath his green hardhat. Red stood shoulder to shoulder with Gary. Gus looked around for Prak and Lok. They crouched in the corner, as far away from Red as they could get. Red tried to catch their attention, elbowing Gary and pointing with his chin, but they were watching Claude. Soon everyone was.

"Now I am sick of this shit," he said. "You guys are fucking up at an ever-increasing rate." His eyes stopped on Red, and he glared.

"What?" said Red, looking around.

"This thing tonight. Not an isolated incident, my fine fucks. Easter is fast approaching. We got a shitload of orders to fill. Now you can suit up and show up, or you can stay the fuck home." Claude put his hands on his hips and waited. "Any questions?" Red raised his hand. When everyone saw the splint, a giddy tension fluttered across the room. For a second, it looked as though Claude would ignore him. But then he threw up his hands and said, "What the fuck is your problem, Red?"

Red waved him off with the splinted finger, the white tape moving in the air like a dainty handkerchief. "Oh, never mind." A few guys laughed quietly.

"No, really, Red, what's on your mind? I got to hear this, because you're really pissing me off lately."

"I'm just curious, Claude." Red pretended to be nervous, like a child asking his father an embarrassing question. "I just wanted to know, Claude. Is it boxers or briefs?"

The break room teetered for a moment as Claude stood on the bench with his mouth open. Then someone let loose a high-pitched gargle, and everything seemed to explode. Even Prak and Lok were laughing. Claude shook his head. Gus read his lips above the noise: Un-fucking-believable. Claude made a little shooing motion with his hand for the guys to start filing out. Then he called after them: "I just hope you all treat Red to the same shit he gives me."

Things settled down quickly, but around dawn, Claude came running into the main work area, his green hardhat slapping his forehead. "Oh, God," he was yelling. He held up a bag of rolls by the twist-tag, spun it in the air like a lasso, and slammed it to the floor. "Oh, Mother of God."

"What now?" Frank said.

"Sons of bitches," Claude screamed. "You're going to kill me." He was talking to the air all around him. The veins in his neck stood out like bungee cords. "Flecks. Flecks. Fucking rust flecks. You hear me? We got flecks in the semibaked oven rolls."

"What's he talking about?" Gus asked Frank.

"Oh, man. Who the hell knows?"

Claude stamped his foot, and his hardhat slid off and bounced on the cement floor. "Some asshole used rusty trays for the semibaked oven rolls." He was standing less than twenty feet away; it took all Gus had to keep from laughing. "Ten thousand bags," Claude said. "And they're shit. You hear me? Shit." Then he stooped to pick up his hardhat. He looked as though he might cry. "We got to pick them clean. There's no other choice. None of you is leaving today till every one of these oven rolls is picked clean."

Frank swore under his breath. "This is unreal."

"Yeah, right," Red yelled. He had stopped stacking hamburger buns. "Give me a break, Claude."

Claude adjusted his hardhat. His hands were shaking. "You're doing it, Red." He pointed his finger with as much force as he could put behind it. "We're not letting an order leave the building like this. There's no time to run a whole new batch. You're doing it like everyone else."

"I'm going home at the end of my shift."

"If I'm doing it, Red, you're doing it."

"Goddamn it." Red slammed his fist into the side of his slicer. "I'm going to miss bird duty."

Half an hour later, the machines were still. A strange quiet filled the bakery. Everyone on third shift sat cross-legged on the floor of the main work area as Prak and another on-call guy wheeled dolly after dolly of semibaked oven rolls into the shop. Red balled up the bread every now and then and lobbed it at Prak's back. Claude yelled at him to knock it off. When Prak was done and dozens of six-foot stacks lined the walls, he found a spot next to his brother on the far side of the room and went to work. They had to pull the rolls, twelve to a pack, out of the plastic, turn each one over in their hands looking for black spots smaller than the head of a thumb tack, pick out the flecks of rust without taking any of the bread, dust the rolls off, and then slide them back into the package. Sometimes Red blew on his, buffing them up with his sleeve.

When guys started arriving for the first day shift, they'd walk into the room and look around in disbelief. Claude barked out what he wanted them to do. Every now and then Red stood up and did a full-body imitation of Claude. But each time he did it, fewer and fewer guys laughed. After a while he stopped.

Gus worked almost all the way through another shift. At three in the afternoon, he called Pam to ask her to stop on her way home from the restaurant. They hadn't had the chance to sleep an entire night through with each other, in the same bed, at the same time, for two months. Even when he'd been on call, they would settle in, and the phone would ring. Claude would be on the other end telling Gus to get his ass down there, stat. When Gus told Pam over the phone that he wouldn't have to be back at the bakery until the next night, she gave him a little cheer.

Then, in that low voice she used when she wanted to sound sexy, she said that they could probably put the time to good use. He saw her chin bunch up. "Right," he said, though all he wanted to do was sleep.

He sat on the curb in front of the bakery to wait for her, his back to the door. It was the beginning of April, but the air was still chilly. Across the way, the gas pumps of a boarded-up Shell station were wrapped in clear plastic sheets that flapped in the breeze. An old Saab without wheels was propped up on cinder blocks. Pigeons heaved and grunted on the ledges of the building above him. He was having a hard time keeping his hands still. They smelled faintly chemical from the raw oven rolls, like formaldehyde. He wondered how many times he'd have to wash them before it would be safe to touch Pam in the tender spots. His fingers kept wanting to turn and pick, and every time he closed his eyes he imagined, with a strange satisfaction, coming across an especially large rust fleck.

The guys from his shift came out of the building behind him in ones and twos and walked off toward the parking lot. He caught scraps of their conversation. Each time it wasn't Red, Gus felt himself getting tenser and tenser. But he stayed where he was. Frank walked out and asked him if he needed a ride. Gus told him no and thanked him. Prak and Lok came out, talking Cambodian, both at the same time, and moved quickly, nervously down the street. Then, a minute later, right behind him, Gus heard someone hawk and spit, and he knew it was Red. Gus didn't turn around. He kept his shoulders hunched, his elbows on his knees.

"Hey, how long you been here?" Red said. Gus made a show of looking left and right, as though surprised.

"About ten minutes."

"Huh?"

"I just sat down."

"Fuck me." Red walked a short way out into the street and stood parallel to Gus. "How long have you been at the goddamn bakery?" Over his work clothes Red wore a stained black and white blazer with a houndstooth check pattern. The sleeves were too short. He couldn't have buttoned it if he'd wanted to.

"A little over two months." Gus's hands were shaking. He tucked them under his armpits.

"Right." Red coughed a couple of times, hawking deeply, and spat again out into the street, as though trying to reach the far curb. "What's your name again?" Gus had never seen Red alone. His face seemed calmer, but the sneer, something about the oily flesh between his eyes and nose, hadn't left him.

"Gus."

Red nodded. "You don't like working here, do you, Gus?"

He didn't know what to say. He pictured Red wearing Claude's green hardhat. "The pay's fine."

"Right, Gus." Red grinned, his eyes on the flapping plastic. "But do I get a sense you're not exactly devoted to the manufacture of bread and bread products?"

"Like I said—"

"Fuck me." When Red walked a short distance up the street, Gus thought their discussion was over. But then Red turned and walked at an angle, like a crab, back to him. "What are you doing right now?"

At first Gus didn't know what he meant. "Waiting for my wife," he said after a pause. "Why?"

"I'm going over and get a beer." He wasn't looking straight at Gus. He was grimacing. "You got time for a beer?"

"Beer?"

"You heard of it?"

"I don't know, Red."

"Come on." Red pointed down the street. "You can sit in the window and watch for her."

Gus was dying for a Labatt's. He found himself getting up and walking with Red, who spat a few more times as he walked a little ahead.

Except for the bartender and two old men shooting pool, the bar was empty. One of the old guys raised his hand silently when he saw Red. He and Gus sat at a corner of the window counter so Gus could look down the street at the front of the bakery. "What do you want?"

"Labatt's, if they have it."

Red raised his eyebrows, got up, and went over to the bar. In a minute or two, he came back with two bottles of Rolling Rock. He sat back down and took a long swig of his beer. Gus was just going along with it, letting the currents take him a little ways out. He had some time to kill.

"How old are you?" Red asked.

"Twenty-eight."

"Which means I been working at the bakery since you were in grammar school."

"Yeah, I guess."

They drank their beers to the crack of the cue ball.

"You got a wife?" Red lifted his chin. "That's right, you're waiting for her."

After a pause Gus said, "You?" He didn't want to be rude.

"What?"

"Got a wife?"

"Fuck no. I live alone."

What kind of woman would marry a guy like Red? Gus wondered. What would you call her, Mrs. Red? "Where?" Gus asked.

"Huh?"

"Where do you live?"

"That trailer park just over the Freetown line?"

Gus nodded. He had no idea where it was.

"The Blue Pines Mobile Village."

"Nice name."

"It's just a little shit hole of a place."

Gus pictured Red's kitchen, his bathroom. He didn't particularly want to.

"You got any kids?" Red asked. His face had changed. He sat more hunched, talking to Gus from the shelter of his shoulders.

"No."

"You're twenty-eight, and you don't have kids yet?"

Gus laughed some air through his nose.

"You trying or what?" Red asked.

Gus looked out the window and shook his head.

"What? Oh, sorry. Is that too fucking personal?"

Gus shrugged.

"Fuck it, then." They drank their beers in silence. Red finished his off. He got up, his stomach scraping the edge of the counter. "Want another?"

"No, thanks."

Red sat down again. "What'd you do before the bakery?"

"House painting."

"No shit. How was that?"

"Fine."

"You work for someone?"

"No. I had my own business."

"That sounds like a fucking great little situation. So what the hell happened?"

Gus didn't say anything. He just shook his head.

"No fucking problem," Red said. "You don't want to talk about it. No skin off my ass, as it were. I was just asking." Tilting the bottle straight up, Red tried to drain the last few drops onto his tongue. "Sure you don't want another?"

"No," Gus said. He wondered whether he should offer to return the favor and buy Red another Rock. "But thanks anyway, Red."

"Come on." Red stood up. "I got something to show you."

"What?"

"My car," he said. "You got to see this car." When Gus parted the curtains again, the Chevette was idling in front of the bakery.

"Thanks." He pointed out the window. "But my wife's here."

"Sure. Good." Red held out his hand for Gus to shake. When Gus didn't take it, Red opened the door. "Say hello to her for me. What's her name?"

Gus squeezed past. He felt funny speaking her name in front of Red. "Pam," he said, finally.

"Right."

"Thanks for the beer, Red."

"Hey, no fucking problem."

Gus left him standing in the entrance to the bar and walked quickly across the street.

"Who the hell was that?" Pam asked when Gus got into the car.

"That?" he said. As they passed him, Red gave a little finger-fluttering wave with his good hand. "Let me put it this way— no one we'd want to invite over for supper."

Red watched the car drive away. "No skin off my ass," he said. He belched loudly and followed the curve of a pigeon as it swooped down from a ledge. Then he walked around the bakery to where his green GTO shone in the afternoon sunlight.

When Gus and Pam pulled into their apartment parking lot, the roofers were standing around the pickup talking with Mr. Medeiros. In his light blue suit, he looked like a television preacher come down from the pulpit to witness to the workingmen. He called over that the roofers were done for the day, and Gus thanked God for such a simple grace. "Thing is, we're going to have to take the whole roof out," one of the workers said. "It's going to take about a week longer. We found some serious rot up there." Gus was too tired to care. He hung onto the hem of Pam's polyester vest as she climbed the stairs. He didn't even take a shower, just stripped off his work whites and slid between the sheets. Pam said she was going back out for something special to cook for him. "You get to sleep," she said. "I'm going to take care of everything. We're going to relax tonight." Gus heard the door scrape shut, and he let himself drift off.

Before he opened his eyes again, he could hear steaks sizzling from the kitchen. A good sweet smell filled the bedroom. It was almost dark outside. He looked over at the clock—7:30. He lay in bed for a minute or two, listening to Pam's footsteps in the kitchen. He could tell she was wearing her slippers. Feeling a little dizzy, he got up and walked naked into the bathroom. He shut the door and looked at himself in the full-length mirror. Fat had gathered at his waist. He was heavier than he'd ever been in his life. He looked at his squashed navel, his shrunken cock, and his balls, one drooping lower than the other. They do that, he reminded himself. That's normal. He thought about the time he'd made love to Pam from behind as they stood in front of the mirror at the old apartment. He was tired, but maybe tonight would be good. Then he ran the shower, testing the stream a few times before he stepped in. Even with the water rushing around him he could smell the broiling steaks.

He came out of the bathroom with a towel around his waist and sat down at the table just like that, naked except for the towel across his lap. "Oooh," Pam said, stroking Gus's leg with the sole of her cold foot. "I like this." She'd set out a dish of sliced tomatoes, a bowl of green beans, and two small salads. Halfway through the meal she remembered the potatoes in the toaster oven. They ate those last. Then they piled the dishes up on the counter and got into bed together. Gus was damn tired. Every time he turned his head too quickly, he saw a hundred flecks of rust. But he knew Pam had been waiting for a long time to settle into something a little more significant than those morning quickies. Sure, he thought, I'm game. I love my wife.

In bed, they slid over each other for a while the way they used to, taking everything slow and feeling the powdery texture of their skin—her on top of him first, then him on her. In the half-light of the room, the freckles on Pam's shoulders and back looked like spattered brown paint. Primer, maybe. When he knew it was time to get down to business, Gus reached under the bed for the box of condoms. He sat up, tore a packet open, pulled out the slippery ring.

"Jesus, I hate those," Pam said.

"You ain't the only one, babe."

"I wish—"

"I know."

Gus unfurled the condom down over his pecker as best he could. But just as he was nestling his hips down in between Pam's thighs again, he thought he heard something far off. "Oh, shit," he said softly.

"What?"

"Nothing." He didn't know why he was whispering.

Pam spread her legs and pulled her knees up with her hands. But just as he was about to enter her, he heard it again —a faint cry that seemed to come from beneath the bed. "What day is it?" he asked her.

"Wednesday." Wakes were usually Tuesdays and Thursdays. It must have been the wind. "Why?" she asked.

"You didn't hear anything?"

"Like what?"

"Wait." They held themselves taut, listening.

"That's nothing," she said, pulling him closer. "Just ignore it."

He covered her mouth with a kiss, and they got under way again. But every time he felt about to come, the tension gathering at the tops of his thighs, he heard the sound again — like an old, tearless Portuguese woman in black.

At work the next night, Claude and Prak were waiting for Gus by the machine. "Frank called in sick," Claude said. He jerked a thumb at Prak. "He knows what to do." Under his apron, Prak wore a sleeveless white T-shirt. His thin arms were veined and sinewy. When Claude walked off, Gus put out his hand, and Prak took it lightly without expression.

"How's it going?" Gus said. "You holding up?" He wondered whether Prak knew who'd come off call first. Prak looked at him from under the visor of his hardhat.

"Good," said Prak.

The belt scraped into motion. The next batch of rolls would be tumbling by soon. Gus snapped on the slicer and waited while it revved into a steady whine.

Across the room, Red looked calm, as he and Gary worked their machine. But every once in a while, he'd lean over and say something to crack Gary up, something Gus couldn't hear above the rumble of the belts. Then he'd look quickly in their direction. Once, Red caught Gus's eye and gave him a short nod. A shiver ran over Gus's scalp. He was getting used to the thought of working under Red in the future, but he didn't want anyone to think they were friends — least of all Prak.

Prak and Gus took their short breaks at separate times. They didn't talk at all. Another on-call guy — some college kid on spring break — spelled them fifteen minutes apart. At the door of the break room Gus met Red coming out. Smiling, Red paused to ask him how things were.

"Not bad," Gus said. He kept his voice as flat as he could.

"So that was your wife, huh? In the car? What was that, an 'eighty-three Chevette?"

"'Eighty-four," Gus said. "Excuse me." He walked over to the Coke machine. Later, he made sure he took his long break well after Red had returned from his.

It was a slow night. Red and Gary finished ahead of them, about an hour and a half before the end of the shift. Red left Gary to dismantle the machine and disappeared. Every time Gus looked over, Gary seemed to be smiling to himself. Gus started to wonder what was up. Red must be doing bird duty, he thought. But he was getting nervous. He stood up on the rungs of the stool and scanned the far ends of the room, searching in a circle until he was looking at Prak, who worked quietly six feet away, stacking and turning the hot dog rolls in two-layered sets of twelve.

Then Gus saw Red.

He was leaning against the wall in the shadow of an I-beam twenty feet behind Prak, twisting something over and over in his hands. When he knew Gus had seen him, Red crunched up his face and put his splinted finger to his lips. It was a plastic bag from his machine's automated bagger. No way, Gus thought. No fucking way. Red shook his head sharply, his eyes narrowing to pencil lines. He mouthed something Gus couldn't fully understand. It was just a gag, Red was saying. A bag gag. Jesus Christ, can't you take a goddamn joke? Gus looked over at Gary, who watched them from a crouch.

Gus didn't know why he hesitated, why he didn't just reach over and tap Prak on the shoulder. Or why he didn't pick up his stool and crack it over Red's flattopped skull. He just watched as Red made his move out of the shadows and slipped the bag over Prak's hardhat and down around his small neck. For a second, Prak stood completely still, as though he'd expected just such an attack, as though ignoring Red was the best way to handle it. But then the rolls were flying off in all directions. Prak's hands flailed back, trying to get a grip on Red's arms, his face, anything. Red laughed. He danced clear, his big gut jellying under his apron.

Gus could see the Cambodian's face through the bag. Prak was looking right at him, his eyes bulging as the plastic billowed out and in with his breathing. "Red, fuck off him," Gus said. Gary stood behind him now, making weird throaty noises. When Gus turned, he saw the slicer jamming up with rolls. They were folding over and into each other like some puckered yellow mouth chewing on itself. When he shoved his right hand in to clear it, his fingers went all numb, and he jerked back with a "shit." But he didn't look at them right away because Prak's brother Lok had wrapped his elbows around Red's face and was clawing at his eyes and screaming in a high-pitched shriek that echoed the screeching of the belt as it shuddered to a stop. Gus held his hand up in the weak light. The slicer had opened a deep diagonal gash across the knuckles. His fingers shivered and twitched. The wound was raw and pulpy, showing bits of yellowish white and dark purple and just now beginning to well over with blood. Gus heard Gary say, "Oh, my fucking word." The room started to tip forward, then back, then up and over, slow and underwater-like. Gus was thinking of Pam's lips on his fingers as he fell off the stool.

• • •

He was lying on his side when he woke up, the chance sounds of the emergency room—voices drawing nearer and passing, a phone ringing—having registered sometime earlier, in a dream in which Claude was calling him in to the bakery. Gus rolled over. He mouth was dry and sticky. From the gurney where he lay, he could see a sunlit parking lot beyond sliding glass doors. There was a strip mall across the street, a line of cars waiting for service at a Taco Bell drive-through, a seagull standing on top of a street lamp. He felt queasy. He lifted himself on his elbows and looked around the room. At the check-in station down the hall, two nurses stood hunched over a clipboard. Nearer by, a guy in a leather vest and pants sat next to the electric doors with his head against the plate-glass window, an ice bag taped above his eye. The guy lowered his chin when he saw Gus looking. "Hey, man."

"What's up?" Gus said.

"Not too much." The guy relaxed his neck again and closed his eyes. "What's up with you?"

Gus's hand was wrapped in gauze up to his wrist, like a white boxing glove. There was a vague throbbing, as though he were clenching and unclenching his fist. One second the hand felt too heavy to lift; the next, it was too light to keep down. A clear plastic tube sloped from a patch of tape on his forearm to an IV bag hanging from a chrome tree. He was wearing a green hospital gown, but underneath, his work pants were crusty and brown with dried blood. He lowered himself again.

Almost immediately, he heard Red's voice echoing along the shiny corridor. Gus sat up and tried to swing his legs over the edge of the gurney, but a wave of dizziness stopped him. A male nurse was pushing Red in a wheelchair. Red's pink belly bulged below his blood-speckled T-shirt. His eyes were wrapped with clean white bandages. He looked like some crazy Indian, his stiff red hair sticking up above the gauze. Gus smiled and nodded his head. Lok had done a job with those fingernails of his. Red was helpless. He couldn't see a thing. Serves the bastard right, Gus thought. But in the next moment, Red's whimpering and the sight of his small white hands sweeping the air in front of him chased the delicious feeling away.

Red's wheelchair caught the edge of a gurney, rattling it into a steel table. Red hunched over, startled. "Motherfucker," he hissed. "What's up with you, hoser?" The nurse rolled his eyes.

Behind them came Gary, his neck jutting forward as he walked, Red's blazer over his arm. His shirt was spotted with Red's blood.

The nurse set the wheelchair across the room from Gus and told Red to wait there until he came back.

"Yeah, right. I thought I'd wheel myself home."

Gary helped Red off with his bloody shirt. Pink and blotchy, his stomach seemed to balance in his lap like some flesh-colored medicine ball. Gary whispered something, but Red kept talking to himself, jerking his flattop back and forth. Sunlight fell across his blue boots.

Finally, Gus turned and eased his legs over the edge of the gurney. "He gonna be all right, Gary?" he called. When Gary saw Gus, he looked worried.

"Now who the fuck is that?" Red asked. His voice was high and thin, almost girlish. Gary patted him on the knee.

"Just Gus," he said quietly.

"Who?"

"Gus," Gary said. "Over on hot dog rolls?"

Gus slid off the gurney and calmly wheeled his chrome IV tree toward them. The far wall seemed to recede slowly as he walked.

"Oh, yeah, Gus," Red said. "Yeah, I know Gus. Sure, we're drinking buddies. We go way the fuck back."

Gus felt a tightening in his bowels. What am I doing? he thought. Why not just turn and walk through the electric door and out into the sunlight and all the way home to Pam? Where is Pam?

"Is he going to be all right?" he asked Gary. "How bad is it?"

"Pretty fucking bad," Red said. Then his voice broke: "Motherfucking Bert." His chin was quivering. He looked as though he might start crying.

Gus stopped where he was. He couldn't believe it. Red was actually blaming Prak. "Take it easy, Red," Gary whispered, but he was looking at Gus with worried eyes.

"Take it easy, my ass."

"It's going to be all right," Gary said.

"Fuck that shit." Red seized the armrests of the wheelchair. "I wish Bert was here right now. The little prick."

Out in the parking lot, a doctor in a lab coat leaned against a green Jaguar as he talked to a woman who was laughing at something he'd said. Gus's heart was working now. A dull ache had begun to flicker somewhere below his wrist, as though he couldn't be sure his own hand was the source of the pain. He turned away from Red and started back to his gurney, but then paused. "You're out of line, Red," he said, facing him again.

Gary glared, shook his head, and motioned Gus back across the room. But it was too late. Red pointed his nose toward Gus. "What did you say?"

"I said, 'You're out of line.' You slipped a goddamn plastic bag over the kid's head. What did you expect?"

Red slammed his fist against the armrest. "Fuck me. I was just screwing around with Bert. Flock or Lok or whatever the brother's name is, he suckered me. That's cheap. That's—"

"Suckered you?" Gus said.

"Damn right," Red said. "What the hell are we talking about? You were sitting right there. You saw the whole goddamn thing."

Gus cocked his head. "You know something, Red?" He tried to cross his arms, but the plastic tube pulled taut, and the IV tree jerked forward, almost toppling to the floor. Gary was waving him off, grimacing now.

"What? Lay it on me, Gus." Red sucked the spittle from his lips. "What you got to say? Am I wrong? You just sat there and watched. Now you're some kind of goddamn choirboy? You're Mother Teresa now? Jesus, I didn't know who I was working with."

Gus felt his shoulder blades shivering now. The room had gone all chilly. He took a deep breath. His wounded hand seemed twice its normal size, light and hollow beneath the bandages, like a balloon on the end of a string.

"And where do you get off, anyway?" Red stood up, the wheelchair rolling back to slam against the wall. Gary fussed with the wheel brakes. Red teetered a little. "Huh? What you got to say?" Red wasn't facing Gus directly; he was talking to the lime green support column four feet away from him. "Why didn't you stand up to me right then and there, you candy-assed motherfucker?"

Gary tried to ease Red back into the chair. "Come on, Red. Take it easy." But Red shoved him off, almost losing his balance.

"No, you take it easy."

Gus looked down at the blood-browned hems of his pant legs. He told himself to step back, get some distance on the situation, like the time he wrecked the van and was sitting next to Homer on the curb with his ankles crossed when the cops came. But it was no good. It had been no good back then either. He tried to inhale deeply again, but his throat seized up. Then, before he could stop himself, he hauled back with his good hand and whacked Red on the side of the head. For a second Red stood very still. He was gasping for air, his pasty white arms hanging loose at his sides. Helpless, Gus thought, and the word was followed by a wave of disgust. So he gave Red another whack. Even as he was doing it, he thought: I never hit anyone before in my life, and here I am starting out with a guy who can't see a thing.

Suddenly, Gus and Red were rolling over each other, loose hands and forearms smacking the floor. Gus's IV had pulled out. It snaked plasma across the tiles as he tried to grate Red's ear against the fluting of a heat vent. Beneath him, Red panted and swore, a confused rush of *fucks* and *shits* and wailing noises that made Gus want to laugh and cry at the same time. The guy with the bag taped to his forehead was on his feet clapping now. "Go, man, kick his ass, yessir." But as he wrangled with Red's flailing arms, Gus couldn't tell which of them the man was rooting for. Then Gary climbed on Gus's back, weaseling his hands under Gus's forearms to break the half nelson he'd managed on Red. When that didn't work, Gary grabbed a fistful of Gus's hair and twisted. "Take it easy, Gus," he kept saying. "Take it easy." Gus jerked his head back into Gary's nose, and Gary rolled off. Now Gus was riding Red's fat belly, clutching him by the throat with his good hand and jabbing him in the face again and again with the bad one, the white bandages reddening from inside and out. Red tried to buck Gus off, his arms whipping, his hands grabbing the air.

The glass doors flew apart, and Pam walked into the emergency room in her Friendly's uniform. Her freckled hands covered her mouth. "Gus," she said. She stepped forward, turned, and walked back out the door. Then, as though remembering something, she hesitated, turned around again. Gus steadied himself atop Red, but seeing her that way, in tears, her chin bunched, her hair back from her face in that pathetic visor they made her wear, he returned to the task at hand. Red was sobbing openly now as Gus grabbed him by the ears and wrung, bouncing his head on the tiles a few times for good measure.

Two security guards and the male nurse stripped Gus away from Red, whose bandages had fallen off, revealing his scratched-up eyes. The whites were bloody, the lids fluttering raw as the irises rolled wildly. The guy in the corner whistled through his teeth. "Oh, man. You fucked him up something fierce." His voice sounded disappointed, almost sad. "Look at his eyes." He clucked his tongue.

"That wasn't me," Gus said, as the nurse slammed him into a chair.

"You stay put, wild man."

"The bastard had it coming," Gus pleaded.

Pam stood on the black electric doormat, staring at Gus in a way he'd never seen before. She looked absolutely terrified.

"Pam," Gus said, standing. "That's Red, the guy I told you about." When he approached her, she stepped backward. The sliding glass doors tried to come together, tried to shut behind her, but they only shuddered halfway, then opened again. "He had it coming, Pam." A few strands of her hair caught the sunlight. "He's a son of a bitch. You should see what he does to those birds."

Which way?" Gary asked.

Red slouched in the passenger seat of Gary's pickup truck. "Where are we?" He took deep breaths, trying not to exhale too loudly. He had quieted himself, but as he directed Gary toward the Blue Pines Mobile Village, his stomach churned and more than once he felt a burning in his throat he had to fight to keep down. He couldn't believe how much of a pussy he'd been back in the emergency room. How he'd whimpered and cried. Fuck! Then he was thinking about what that lady doctor had told him, that the eye patches would be on for at least a month and that she'd make a decision then about Red's severely scratched corneas.

They drove for fifteen minutes before Red heard the popping of the gravel lane and he knew Gary had pulled into the trailer park. He felt the sun on the right side of his face.

"Which one?" Gary asked. He hadn't spoken more than two words at a time the whole way there.

"It's the fifth unit on the right. There's a green carport." Red heard the Smayle brothers' dog bark twice. He wondered who was watching him.

"I see it," Gary said.

Gary helped Red out of the truck, guiding him up the two steps, through the door, and into a kitchen chair. "Is this OK?"

"Yeah. Fine."

"OK," Gary said, backing toward the door. "So I'll drop your car off after work tonight. My wife will follow me over."

"Whoa, where're you going? You want a sandwich or something?"

"Oh, no, thanks." Gary patted him on the shoulder. The gesture startled Red. "You want me to talk to Claude tonight when I see him?"

"Tell him I'll call in."

"Right." Gary paused with his hand on the doorknob.

"Hey, what the fuck? Stick around," Red said. "You want a beer or something?"

"No, thanks, Red. I got to get home, get to bed."

"Anything—glass of water?"

"All right."

"Above the sink."

Gary took down a coffee mug and filled it halfway at the tap. "You want something?"

"How about a beer?" Red said. "You mind getting me a beer?"

Gary snorted. "No problem." He took a Rolling Rock out of the refrigerator and twisted off the cap. Then he fitted the bottle into Red's outstretched palm.

"Sure you don't want one?" Red asked.

"I don't drink before noon."

Red took a sip. "What the hell time is it?"

"Quarter till," Gary said. Then, after a long pause: "You want me to call someone for you?" Red knew the question had been coming. He took another sip of beer. He couldn't think of a soul. A cousin lived in Boston, but they hadn't talked for five years. For a second he thought of Leticia, the woman two trailers down.

"No. That's all right, Gary." The name hung in the air. During the eight years they'd worked together, Red had never used it.

"So I guess I'll check in when I drop the car off." Gary put his cup in the sink. He hadn't drunk from it. "Right. Tomorrow morning."

He left, the screen door clapping shut behind him.

Red finished his beer. A dog barked in the distance. He moved his head left, then right, as though surveying the length of the trailer. "Fuck," he said aloud. But the quiet of the room seemed to swallow up his voice. Finally, he stood and felt around in the air for the table, inching himself along by its curve to the sink and then, by the edge of the counter, to the cool metal surface of the refrigerator. He opened the door and groped for another beer. He twisted off the top and drank it where he stood. When he was done, he paused, squeezing the bottle in his fist and thinking whether he would smash it against the wall or not. He put the bottle down on the counter and moved slowly toward the bedroom, his feet shuffling along the worn carpeting. Carefully, he undressed and lowered himself onto the waterbed.

Red woke late in the afternoon to the sound of people talking. Mrs. Souza and Leticia were discussing Leticia's kids and the Smayles' motorcycles and the dust that sometimes rose from the park lanes and powdered their furniture. Then, suddenly, they were talking about him. "I saw this guy, over here, walking back from your place on Wednesday night," said Mrs. Souza.

He heard a whisper.

"No, his car's gone."

"It was strange," said Leticia. He could tell she was smiling. "No doubt about it."

"He's strange."

"He brought over a linguiça sandwich. Out of the blue, there's this weird guy I don't know standing at my door with a linguiça sandwich."

They laughed.

"I think he's harmless, though," Mrs. Souza said. "But he gives me the creeps."

"No kidding."

Red imagined the look on their faces when he stepped out onto his deck and told them to go get fucked. But instead he turned onto his side, the water shifting quietly beneath him. He tried to think of something else. He ran his palm over the rough gauze bandage around his face, then fingered the corners of his flattop. He wondered if his hearing would improve now that he couldn't see. He wondered if he'd be able to sleep that night and who would take over bird duty for him at the bakery.

• • •

On the drive home, Gus hung his arm in the breeze to cool his wound. As they moved beneath the latticed shadow of the Fairhaven–New Bedford bridge, he tried to take Pam's hand in his good one, but she pulled away and gripped the steering wheel tightly.

"I didn't even know you," she said, shooting him a glance.

"You know me."

"You told me you never hit anyone before."

"I hadn't."

"You were really hurting him, Gus." Pam squeezed the wheel. "His face was all bloodied up."

Gus snorted, shrugged.

"It's a joke?" she said. "Hurting people like that? You looked like you were having fun."

"You don't know Red."

"No." She shook her chin, a little at first, but then she was wagging her head. "And I don't know you."

"Pam, you know me."

They passed a Greek restaurant he and Homer had painted a year before. The lilac finish on the south side of the building had begun to blister and crisp away. Gus remembered warning the owner about skimping with the cheaper latex paints, but she'd given him a choice—he could do it her way, or he could walk.

In the parking lot of the funeral home, the roofers were sitting on the lowered tailgate of their pickup eating pizza. Gus and Pam got out of the Chevette. "Holy shit," one of them called. "What happened to you?"

Gus smiled. "Mosquito bite." Then he went into a boxing stance, jabbing the air with the wrapped fist. The roofers laughed. He followed Pam into the building.

Upstairs, Pam rushed into the bathroom and closed the door. Gus walked into the living room. He sat down and snapped on the TV for a few seconds, then turned it off. He got up and went back to the bathroom door. He knocked.

"No," Pam said.

"Come out, Pam." His lips touched the wood. "I'm still the same Gus."

"I don't know about that."

He knocked again. "Please."

"Stand back," she said after a pause.

"Jesus, Pam. What's the problem?"

She opened the door a little first, looking at him through the crack, then opened wider. Gus wrapped his good arm around her waist, pressed up against her, and ran the tip of his tongue along her neck. Her skin tasted faintly of hamburger grease. He felt good now. The pain in his hand—a pulsing, fuzzy blue light—was like some new energy source. Something had come over him.

"Wait," she said, squirming out of his hold. "I have to think this through."

"Pam, it's all right," he said. "I'm all done at the bakery. Fuck it. We got all day and night together. I'm not going back there. I'll find something else."

"Like what? You can't drive. Your hand's a mess."

"Who gives a shit?" he said, smiling. "Let's fuck. Let's do it in front of the mirror."

He moved forward and slipped his arm around her again, this time kissing her hard on the mouth, the way he knew she liked it—sometimes. But she pushed him back. "I got to go."

"What? Where?"

"I don't know. For a ride. Maybe back to work. I can't afford to lose that job."

"Oh, fuck, that's bullshit, Pam." The pounding exploded in a hail of hammering above them. "Son of a bitch," Gus said, looking up. The banging seemed to come in three waves, like a ragged echo. "I don't give a shit, Pam. Let's get in bed."

She shouldered her purse. She hadn't taken her jacket off. "I'll be back." She leaned forward to kiss him, but stopped short, seeming to think twice about it. He tried to hold her, but she pushed him away. From the top of the stairs, he watched her descend. Then he moved to the window and saw her get into the Chevette and drive away.

"Fuck," he said.

He stripped away his bloody work whites and stuffed the clothes into the trash, cramming them down with his foot. Then he went into the bathroom and shut the door. He washed his face, the cold water leaving him breathless. He soaped up his good hand, twisting the bar over and over again in his palm. He stood back, naked in front of the full-length mirror that hung behind the door, and began to slide his fist up and down his cock, moving his hips, keeping time with the rhythm of the hammering above. It didn't take long. He came in a single burst, almost painful, then quickly washed off and put on his jeans and a T-shirt. He walked down the stairs and over to the R & P Tavern.

The place was dark and empty except for the bartender, who was shuffling in and out of the back with cases of beer. The TV over the bar bathed the room in blue light. On the screen, a pregnant meteorologist swept her arm across a weather map. She was talking, but the sound had been turned way down. Gus ordered a sixteen-ounce bottle of Budweiser.

"Where you been?" the bartender asked.

Gus didn't answer.

"What's with the hand?"

Gus took a nice long swig, and his dry throat seemed to loosen. He could breathe now. He told himself to start off slowly—he wasn't going anywhere—pace himself, one bottle, maybe two an hour. He studied the jet stream and the movement of high and low pressure systems on the silent TV. Occasionally, in the mirror across the bar, he watched the roofers bounce up and down the long aluminum ladders. They could pound till they dropped. He didn't care.

Later, hours after they'd left for the day, Gus walked as straight as he could across the street. In tight groups of two and three, people were coming out of the funeral home and getting into their cars.

Upstairs, Pam was already in bed. She was reading a book from one of the courses she'd never finished, the lamp on the bed stand casting a yellowy light around her. Gus dipped to read the cover: *Ralph Waldo Emerson's Collected Essays*. He began to undress quietly.

"I can't sleep with you, Gus," she said without looking at him.

"Pam."

"Please," she said. He swooned a little, and she saw he was drunk. "I don't believe it. You're shitfaced."

"Pam," he started again. He wanted her to know what had happened, that she'd come into the emergency room at the wrong time, that he'd had his reasons for pounding the shit out of Red. But just imagining the effort seemed to exhaust him. He took his pillow and walked out to the living room couch.

At two-thirty in the morning, about the time of midshift break, he woke up. The light of a half-moon fell in stripes through the venetian blinds. His hand was on fire now. Standing naked in the middle of the room, he was cold, but he didn't care. He was suddenly wide awake. He went out into the stairwell. It was even colder there. The sockets of his eyes throbbed almost as badly as his hand, but the buzz still lingered. The hatch to the attic was in the ceiling over the top landing, half a flight up from their apartment. The door lowered with a pull on a short string, and a small wooden ladder unfolded almost to the floor. Cold air tumbled down into his face as he climbed the rickety steps in his bare feet.

Standing on the rough floorboards of the attic, he didn't realize at first that the roof was gone, that he was standing outside, the night sky above him, the moon coating everything with a pale green glow. Bits of torn insulation fluttered in the breeze.

When he and Pam had moved in, they'd put everything they couldn't fit into the apartment up here—four cheap folding chairs that went with a card table, a box spring and frame, the crib his father had given them when they were thinking of having kids. Gus had slept in that crib himself. In one corner was a small desk-and-chair set he'd used for homework in grammar school. A coarse black dust covered it all. He felt it under his feet. As his eyes adjusted to the dark, he saw small black shapes hunched along the edge of the floor, squatting and rocking in the wind. They must be birds, Gus thought. Birds don't fly at night. They find a safe place to roost and settle in. With his good hand, he pulled the desk into the center of the floor and turned it to face north, the darkest part of the sky. The lights of New Bedford glimmered across the river. He wedged himself into the chair. Creaking with his weight, it felt small and wobbly underneath him.

Fun with Mammals

MOTHER'S DAY in the Year of the Rat, and I'm riding
shotgun for my brother-in-law Phil in a borrowed flatbed
semi as we throttle north on Interstate 91 toward Canada,
but instead of packing a firearm, I'm trying to keep a wine cork
on the tip of a nine-inch hypodermic, just in case the narwhal
wakes up ahead of schedule. Bill, our father-in-law, is riding
out back, because someone has to keep the whale's porcelain-
smooth flesh from getting chapped in the breeze. He's got a
fifty-five-gallon drum of saltwater Phil mixed up that he's
ladling from. Occasionally, udder balm must needs be applied.
Bill drew the short match, and I have every confidence in him.
Sometimes in the rearview I can see him tucking a corner of
the blue tarp back under a bit of those three thousand pounds
of gelatinous, mottled blubber as it hangs over the edge of the
bed. This particular leviathan's got a small, small face, eyes
rolled back in its tiny head. And of course who could forget the
magnificent horn? Phil took great care strapping the beast
down to the flatbed as it slept. Getting him—or her, I can't tell
—out of the tank and up there was a whole other story, which

Phil has yet to tell us. When Bill and I showed up, he had the whale already loaded and was sitting in the cab sweating, with the motor running.

Phil's the worst lawyer I have ever known. He puts in the minimum number of hours per week to get by. He gets distracted in the courtroom and has to excuse himself to urinate two, three times a session. His closing arguments are a nightmare, great dissociative works of stream of consciousness punctuated by an occasional *moreover!* or *thus!* It's the stress. He sweats buckets. He gets migraines, his shirts and ties absolutely soaked. I watched one of his cross-examinations once. He was leaving damp footprints all over the courtroom. The judge was speechless. To his credit, Phil has done his best to get past all of this: he's tried primal screams, yoga, high-protein diets, even self-hypnosis—and then he decided to return to just plain heavy drinking.

Last week, he was defending a client accused of smuggling narcotics into the country when *poof!*—the guy turned up missing from his palace in Westport, Connecticut. Phil thought other members of the cartel were worried he'd turn state's evidence. Wherever the man had disappeared to, Phil was relieved—no need for another court appearance now. But the narwhal would have died. The drug guy had it in a blue underground tank so he could watch it through his transparent bedroom wall while he made love. "It makes sense," said Phil. I'm still not sure what he meant. Then there was nobody around to feed the damn thing—upwards of three hundred pounds of mackerel per diem. It had already lost a few dress sizes. That crunched-up face smiling through the thick glass of the tank first thing in the morning. Clicks and little whirs of loneliness, now that the master was gone. So Phil comes up with this no-brainer. One of his golf buddies' firms is handling the bankruptcy case of something called an oceanarium in Nova Scotia. Phil figures if he can get the narwhal there inside of twenty-four hours, he'll just out-and-out give it to them as a donation (he's the de facto executor of the drug dealer's will), claim a huge tax deduction, and save the day for the failing oceanic institution. "That thing's adorable," he said as we drove off. "It's got to be worth big, big bucks. And I'm *giving* it away. I'm handing it over, gratis. All for the children of eastern Canada!"

That was four hours ago, and we're making good time into southern Vermont.

"You should have seen how small Earl was," Phil says, after long silence. Suddenly, I notice Phil's way nervous. Serious sweating has commenced.

"Who's Earl?" I ask. I take a glance in the mirror. "Hey, I can't see Bill."

"*Who's Earl?* The guy who owns Babu." Phil takes a swig from a chrome hip flask. "The guy who *owned* Babu."

"Who the hell's Babu?"

"Babu, the narwhal?" says Phil. "Hello?"

"Can you see Bill on your side?"

Phil thrusts his head out the window, his shoulder-length hair having come undone from its ponytail and whipping madly now around his face. He takes the opportunity to examine his teeth in the semi's big rearview mirror. Then he looks back. "Jesus, Babu's fluke is hanging off the side!"

"Yeah, but where's Bill?" I ask. Phil applies the brakes and begins shifting gears like a lunatic. I can see the trailer fishtailing behind us. "Easy!" I say. "You don't even have a license to drive one of these."

Phil shoots me a glance. "Always so technical," he says. "So *negative*. This isn't about me or you. It's about Babu!" He winces as the trailer's rear end takes out a hundred feet of guardrail and we come to a halt. "There we go! That's beautiful! Satisfied now?" He jumps out of the cab and I follow.

Out back there's nothing left of the salt stew Bill was ladling onto Babu with a small shovel. But we do locate Bill himself, who lies wedged up against the cab, still alive, but with one of his legs seeming to disappear into the creamy blubber that is Babu. Babu has rolled over on top of him.

Phil struggles to push the narwhal's fluke back onto the

flatbed. "Bill, I don't see the udder balm." He throws up his hands. "Look! Babu's skin is all rough here, and here. Look at this dorsal fin! Bill, excuse me, but what the hell have you been doing for the last three hours?"

Bill is slicked with a thick layer of what appears to be whale mucus. "Sorry, Phil, but the wind, well, it was whipping pretty strong once you got to the interstate." I've never heard Bill raise his voice above the hushed monotone in which he communicates with—what I can only term the *outside world.* He's retired. "But not from life," he often whispers. He refuses to let things bother him. His is a stoicism born of either outright raving madness or a species of genius, the residue of some life-altering encounter with a yawning abyss.

"Come on, Bill!" Phil looks at his naked wrist. "Where are we?" I run to the cab and return with the road map.

"We're making good time," I tell him.

He ignores me. "Has Babu been moving or . . ." Cars scream past. Phil can't seem to find the word.

I lift Bill to his feet. "Or what, Phil?"

"Moving, you know, by itself."

"Like breathing?" Bill asks.

Phil nods.

"Yeah, there's been breathing," says Bill. "I'd direct your attention to the blowhole."

Phil pulls back the blue tarp. The narwhal's horn is sandwiched between two huge pieces of flaking white Styrofoam held together with duct tape. "Oh, yeah," says Phil. "See it working there, the little flap?" He pauses. "What I mean is, has there been there any other, you know, *movement?*"

Bill shakes his head. "No, Phil, no other movement." His suit and tie are utterly ruined. But he's out to help. He wants to do his part. "Though it's been hard to tell, like I said, because of the—"

"Wind? Yeah, thanks, Bill. That's all for now. You want to ride up front? I think it's time for Pete to spend some QT with Babu. Do you mind, Pete?"

I must admit I feel a little dizzy over the task ahead. "No, not at all," I say. But I do insist on lunch. I'm not tending narwhal on an empty stomach.

"Pete," Phil says, "timewise, we're certainly up against it." He wipes a sleeve across his forehead. He looks around. In the wind, the ragged blue tarp slaps at Babu. "Oh, all right. Next exit. An X-Mart or something. Can you live with a Clif Bar?"

"Phil, a fistful of nuts, anything."

"I'm a little hungry myself," whispers Bill.

Phil's suddenly beside himself. "Well, hell, we're not having a sit-down meal, guys! Is that clear? Let's get this thing in motion!"

From the flatbed, I witness Phil's agonizing ascent through the gears, the accordioned guardrail coming loose from the rear axle with a sound like horrendous reptilian screeching in deafening slow-mo. Down the exit to a busy intersection we go. Phil swings the rig out into the traffic, and the motorists waiting at the red light barely escape being clipped by the rear wheels of the trailer. Moments later, driving into a Cumberland Farms parking lot, we nick a corner of the fuel kiosk, which falls to the asphalt while I try to act nonchalant, jouncing with my ankles crossed as I lounge atop Babu.

"OK. Go!" I hear Phil call from the cab. "Get me a six of Dew if they've got it. Warm, please!"

Inside, people are plastered to the windows. It's like that diner scene from *The Birds*. They move aside as I enter. Hushed voices. A small boy is crying in his mother's arms. "That's all right now," she says, glaring over his red hair. "That man's not going to hurt you."

"Far from it," I say. "Tell him." Then, for no reason I can discern, I whisper: "I'm the man from U.N.C.L.E."

"What's that under the plastic out there?" the cashier asks, as I lay out my hastily gotten booty on the counter.

"What?" I don't turn around. "Under that plastic out there? You're standing there asking what's out under that tarp? Is that what you want to know?"

"Yeah, what's that mound you rode in on? You smell like fish."

I look him up and down. "And that's bad?" I ask.

I feel all their eyes on me, my wet ass, all the way out to the rig. But then I realize I've forgotten something and have to go back.

"What the hell do you want now?" the cashier says.

"Do you carry udder balm?" I ask, without missing a beat.

He just snorts and shakes his head.

"Right." I take my sweet time leaving. I meet the eyes of each customer in the place. "I didn't think so."

Outside, I mount Babu again, and as we pull away, I give the crowd a little stiff-wristed Elizabethan wave, then fall ravenously on my bag of unsalted sunflower seeds.

The afternoon passes without incident.

Around dinnertime or so, however, events take a darker turn. A quarter of a mile behind us, a Vermont state trooper is keeping pace. What's more, I think I detect the first indications that Babu may be rousing from slumber. I'm feeling slight *movements*—there's no other way to say it. I knock a few times on the roof of the cab.

"What!" Phil screams out his window.

"Something's amiss with Babu!" I yell.

"Amiss?"

"Babu's waking up!"

Phil takes the next exit at fifty miles per hour—he's learning not to downshift too soon—and Babu slides off almost completely onto the road. We pull into an empty commuter lot surrounded by pine trees. Up on the interstate, the trooper passes without slowing.

Phil's out of the cab in a second. "Pete! Look at Babu! For God's sake, he's hanging off again! What's with you guys? Can you show a little effort?"

I slide off the whale. "I'm pretty sure Babu's waking up."

Just then Babu begins to flop like a hooked bass in the bottom of a boat. It would be comical, if we weren't all covered in narwhal slime as a result.

"Pete, how did it get to this point? I gave you simple instructions. You were supposed to inject at the faintest *hint* of Babu's stirring."

"I know, Phil, but . . ." I look over at Bill, who nods placidly in stoical solidarity.

And now, words nearly fail me as I recount for you, dear reader, the ensuing events. Indeed, we begin to notice certain movements traveling along the soft white underbelly of Babu.

Bill clears his throat. "Phil," he says, "is Babu a lady whale?"

Phil's turning left and right, grimacing, twitching, his hands in his hair. He's trying to act nonchalant, trying not to sweat. "Jesus, what kind of a question is that, Bill?" He takes a swig from his chrome flask. "What's your point?"

"I ask because I think what's happening could very well be whale birth," says Bill. Then, quietly as ever: "Behold, a sentient being is emerging into the world."

Phil throws down the flask. "Dammit! That's not it!" He hoists himself onto the flatbed next to the writhing whale. "Hand me that hypo, will you?"

I run to cab for the needle, come back, and pass it up to Phil, at which point he proceeds, riding the bucking narwhal like some demented prophet, to deliver the last dose of sedative through Babu's thick flesh. Slowly, the whale falls off to sleep.

And yet the movements do not completely cease.

"Aw, hell." Phil leaps from Babu. "Pete, come up here." I climb onto the flatbed. He takes a deep breath with his eyes closed, counts to five, then reaches into the birthing canal of the sedated cetacean and begins rooting around for a time with his head facing away. "All right now," he says and starts to pull. "There we go. OK."

At first I don't believe what I think I'm seeing: two bright blue New Balance running shoes glistening in the failing light of evening. Phil's got hold of one of them, twisting it, yanking it. "Mother of God!" he yells. "Everything's going wrong today! What else can happen? Somebody tell me." He whistles sharply. "Guys, do I have to issue a formal invitation? Help me out here, will you?" Bill takes hold of a protruding ankle and I grab the other sneaker. Phil gets down on his knees and begins massaging Babu's great abdomen from front to back as we pull and pull and pull. Sure enough, slowly our labor bears fruit. We succeed in extracting from Babu's interior a small man, who now lies panting on the flatbed beside us.

"All right, guys, here's the deal." Phil stands up and wipes his hands on his back pockets. "I want you to meet my client, Earl."

Bill and I exchange pleasantries with the man, who's wearing relaxed-fit jeans and the top of a wetsuit two sizes too small. He's a little shaky, sure, and completely covered with slime, but who's going to hold that against him? He removes the scuba mask and snorkel he's been wearing. It seems that the small tube that he was breathing through, the one running from the snorkel into Babu's blubber and then out into the vast ocean of air we all take for granted, must have become partially occluded in the recent rumble up on the highway, and it was all Earl could do to signal his distress to the outside world. Seems Earl was hoping to make it to Canada alive, but here he stands, still in the USA, reduced to nothing more than a pathetic incarnation of his own twisted tradecraft.

A few moments of shared silence pass, and then it's as though I myself wake up and realize where I am. "This is all well and good, but what about our friend Babu?" I say. "What now?" All three are looking at me in wonderment. "Let's get a move on. We need to get this narwhal to the sea, and I mean now."

Once I've sounded the alarum, to a man we begin to scramble, even Earl. Phil meets me at the cab. "Hold on there," I say, talking out of my mind, barking orders like a drill sergeant. "You stick with Babu and your client. I'm driving this rig now. I'm taking charge."

Phil obeys without a word.

And so we strike out due east through the humid May night into New Hampshire. Bill assumes responsibility for navigation, staring for hours at the maps by the light of a little flashlight held in his teeth and consulting a military compass, and it isn't long before the road signs begin intermittently to include words like *beach* and *neck*. With a pink Magic Marker, he circles what he thinks is a pier on the map, but when we get there, it's just barely wide enough to accommodate the full girth of the semi, and I stop the rig and we jump down and join the boys in the back.

Our vigil begins. We will wait for the narwhal to wake. Earl lights a small fire on the flatbed with driftwood, and we watch the flames cast shuddering shadows on the whale's shiny skin. Hours pass. Bill and Earl begin a game of chess with a small magnetic set they find in the rig's glove compartment. We listen to the hiss of the waves. And we wait. All the while I'm thinking that when Babu comes to life, someone's got to barrel-ass the whole goddamn kit and caboodle down the pier and into the foaming brine. And I realize that that somebody's going to be me. I didn't seek out this fate, but I'll be damned if I'm going to shun it now that it's been thrust upon me.

If only Babu would wake up! We remove the makeshift Styrofoam clamp from her horn. Pressing my ear to her abdomen, I listen for a heartbeat among the deep gurgling and popping noises. And I'm thinking someone's got to ride out back, to guide Babu safely into the Atlantic once the rig begins to sink. Someone who can swim.

But we haven't gotten that responsibility assigned, we haven't thought it through as it should be thought through, haven't imagined all the imaginables, plumbed the possible downsides, foreseen the dangers, assessed the risks, quantified the intangibles, or reasoned out the effects, before Babu, her great bulk undulant and crying out for the healing salve of the sea, begins to stir.

Spectator Sport

I VOLUNTEERED to visit insane people at a mental hospital. I was in college. I thought it might be fun. Every Monday after supper I boarded a school bus with ten other students. We drove through burnt-out factory towns, past mills that had once made thread. The whole point was for us to go give the insane some time off from a forty-hour week of groaning and shuffling around in their pajamas.

At the hospital they kept the men and the women separate. I suppose you have to do such things. During our visits we never saw the women. Nor did I complain about that. We met with the men in a huge room that had little furniture and some wire mesh over the windows. Someone in authority had put up the same paint-by-number rural scene on all four walls, in frames that were screwed into the plaster. I noticed that the paintings, upon closer inspection, were actually puzzles.

Blue smoke would drift out of a small side room where the insane smoked. They let them smoke. When they weren't smoking, they were moving about absently through the smoke. *Devoid of intent and purpose* is a phrase that comes to mind. One or two of them were always sitting beneath a black-and-white television mounted high on a wall. No sound, just the pictures. Bottles of liquid soap spinning into view. Common objects changing into shinier common objects. White people's faces getting happier for reasons unknown.

On the first day, the director had stood up in the bus on the way down and warned us not to take the "commitment" lightly. You miss a week, she said, swaying with the movement of the bus, and one of them might "snap." I liked the director. She was the main reason I had volunteered to befriend insane people in the first place. She had shorn most of her hair away, except for a tuft up front, which she dyed a different color each week. She wore a sleeveless T-shirt and a tie-dyed dress and genuine Marine combat boots. Moreover, she wore earrings in the many fleshy parts of her body.

I sensed that the inmates were confused by the director. She reminded them of something. I did not know what. This Mexican insane guy named Pablo became attracted to the director and began to follow her around in his pajamas.

"Te quiero," he often said. "Te quiero."

The director made it known that she wanted me to get between her and Pablo. For two weeks, that was my function. Anytime Pablo and she were in the same room, she required my services as a moving wall.

Most weeks Zeke and I played pool the whole two hours. There was nothing else for me to do. I had lost interest in the mingling. Zeke beat me at nine ball. It made me wonder why he was even in there. I was full of assumptions. I was equating sanity with skill at billiards. He was just this normal auto-mechanic-looking guy in the middle of an absolute horror show. I would shun the others—just ignore them—even though this defeated the very purpose of my being there, which was to make conversation with a wide *variety* of insane people. Two hours per week. It wasn't much to ask.

They annoyed me. You would be into a discussion, thinking, *Hey, OK, not bad, I am actually talking to this lunatic.* Then you would notice that the very same person had begun drooling. Maybe his eyes were rolling back in his head. From there, the discussion would start to lag. Others among the population would simply not leave you alone. A tall Fred Gwynn–looking fellow had heard somehow that I was an English major, even though I myself had not volunteered any such information. Consequently, he felt the need to quote T. S. Eliot every ten minutes or so. He would interrupt his quality downtime to seek me out. I know I should have felt special. He said he had attended Harvard University, the one "just north of Boston." I told him I knew of it.

I was pretty certain Zeke had never heard of T. S. Eliot.

One Monday he—Zeke—and I were shooting pool. I was ignoring the rest of the clientele when this totally new insane guy walked up to the table. He came out of the blue smoke and put two quarters down on the edge of the table. I looked at Zeke. Billiards was free here. Billiards was one of the perks. Quarters did not figure into the current billiards situation. Zeke shook his head. Inexplicably, he looked under the table and then shot me a sidelong glance. He winked. We had become like friends, me and an insane fellow.

The new guy was among the more muscular members of the insane community. He had black hair reminiscent of something from the realm of science fiction. It was sculpted. It had sheen, substance. I thought, *Hey, at least he has not let his hair go. Good for him.*

When the new guy picked up a cue and started sinking Zeke's balls, I felt I must say something. I said, "OK. Easy now." He looked at me. Or, rather, he looked past my right ear, as though he were following the movements of some small hovering object just behind me. Zeke sighed and shook his head again.

I asked the new guy if he wanted to play pool. It was not a particularly intelligent question.

He said, in the voice of a five-year-old child, "Yes, I would." Even though Zeke and I were right in the middle of the rubber game, I was willing to step aside, forgo my own pleasures. For an insane person. It was why I was there. I nodded to Zeke. "Very well," I said. I bowed with a flourish and moved toward one of the green and chrome chairs.

"No," the new guy said. "With you." He pointed his stick at my chest.

"If you insist," I said. Suddenly I was behaving like some maitre d'. The plan? Quickly to defeat and to dispatch him and to get back to my game with Zeke. "Do you mind terribly?" I asked Zeke. Zeke shrugged his melancholy shrug.

Then, for no real reason, I imitated the Duke—that is, John Wayne—something along the lines of "Well, why don't you just rack them up, pilgrim?" Impressions are a mistake in a mental hospital. The new guy was baffled. He began to grin wildly and move from side to side. He was saying something I did not understand, spraying bits of foam in all directions. I surveyed the room. Others had noticed us. The director watched me from her own green and chrome chair on the far wall. Her tuft was the color of insulation this week. She did not return my smile.

Zeke sat down and fixed his eyes on the floor three feet in front of him. He was a true fan of billiards, but pool, went the look on his face, is not a spectator sport.

The new guy had trouble with the rack and could not seem to align the balls with anything close to satisfactory precision. He kept changing the order of solids and stripes in the triangle. He'd step back for a long view, then change more balls. After a few minutes of this, I offered my assistance. "Excuse me." Smiling, I waited for him to stand aside. "Allow me." I gave the rack a shake, rolled it in a wide circle, and then I made a big scientific deal of setting the tip of the triangle on the white dot. I crouched to get a better angle. If I'd had a tape measure, I would have used it. "What do you think?" I asked. "Are we good?" The new guy nodded his head, panting. From her green chair across the room, the director continued to watch me. "Why don't you break?" I said.

He laughed.

After breaking, he got his choice. His first shot was astounding, a combination that began with the cue ball skipping over the eight and ended with a subtle kiss that toppled a solid into the corner pocket. From there, he sank balls with ease, moving to each new position before they had come to rest. He crouched occasionally to line up shots. The guy was putting on a clinic right there in our midst. Zeke was paying attention now.

When the new guy finished off the stripes, he started in on mine without hesitation. "Easy," I said. But he waved me off. I looked to Zeke. He did not know what to do. "I think you might be sinking my balls," I said, tentatively. The new guy ignored my comment. He was insane and could not be bothered. The sharp marbly crack of the cue ball had attracted a small crowd to the table, maybe half a dozen. My Harvard friend, Gwynn, held an unlit pipe. He smiled at me with a line of *Prufrock* on his trembling lips. Even Pablo was there, slowly rubbing his fingers together.

In minutes, the new guy had cleared the table, except for the eight ball. He took his time getting a bead. His hair once again captivated my imagination. Glazed by the overhead light bulbs, it seemed almost edible, a delicious treat on display for bakery patrons. Then he attempted an absurd and wholly unnecessary triple bank shot that almost worked out. The mental cases all around me groaned. Without a word, he straightened up and handed me his cue stick. He wanted me to shoot. He had left me with a patsy shot—just a tap and the eight ball would be sunk. I hesitated. "My turn?" I asked. The new guy made a face and grunted. Of course. He shoved the stick at me angrily. I surveyed the crowd. Then, as I took the cue, Gwynn bent in close to me.

"A-ha," he whispered. "Do I dare to eat a peach?" I gave him a quick look over my shoulder. His eyes were wide, his breath absolutely horrendous.

I turned back to the table. The new guy's jaw was moving slowly. I gave serious consideration to missing the shot on purpose. I could hit it too hard and pop it right back out, I thought. I could chalk it up to a bit of showboating gone bad. But patronize him I would not. On the bus, the director had told us to treat the insane as we ourselves—were we of unsound mind—would want to be treated. Damn straight. Besides, if I missed, Gwynn would not let me live it down. It would be *The Waste Land* for weeks—"HURRY UP PLEASE IT'S TIME," in a shrill woman's voice. And then Zeke and the new guy would be racking up the table, and I'd be on the sidelines watching two lunatics play pool. So I bent. I bent and I took careful measure. I false-cocked the cue a few strokes. Smoke curled around my ankles. There was unhealthy breathing somewhere in the silence. Then, with some élan, I snapped the black ball cleanly into the side pocket. A cheer went up from the small crowd. Huzzah! Someone slapped my back. Zeke was on his feet behind me. "OK, you win," he said, reaching for a cue stick. "Let's rack them up."

I turned to the new guy and extended my hand across the corner of the table. I was the very image of a really civil sane guy. "Thanks for the game," I said. "You shot well." He didn't move, just stood there regarding my hand as though it were a hunk of putrid cheese. His forehead was crawling, crawling and bulging all over.

"How's that?" he said. He shut his eyes tight. "You say you won?" He kept shaking his head, like someone emerging from under water. "Come again."

I shrugged, a bad imitation of Zeke.

The new guy grimaced, the tendons in his neck tensing. "Come again?" he kept saying. "Come again?"

The more he said it, the more the room became charged with fear, or that dizzy feeling just before fear takes over. Off in their cubicles, the nurses did not seem to notice. *What the hell good are they?* I was thinking. Nor could I locate the director.

"What did he say?" The new guy was pointing at Zeke but looking at me. "Did he say you won?"

"Delightful," Gwynn whispered, "simply delightful."

"Yeah, that's what I said." Zeke was impatiently gathering balls from the cracked leather pockets. "He tried to tell you you were sinking his balls." He set the rack down a little too hard. "You wouldn't listen, would you?" And then without looking up: "I guess that's life."

The new guy's biceps started jumping like mammals in a bag.

"OK, look," I said. I had my hands out at my sides. Something told me this was what you did around muscular insane people. You put your hands out at your sides, palms open, and you smiled. And you spoke very slowly. "Something got lost in translation," I said. "It can happen. There was obviously some confusion. We'll call it a draw."

His eyes had retreated under his enormous brows. "Back off, fucker," he snarled. So in this case, I reasoned, what you did was spread your arms out even more.

"OK, man, you're one up on me," I said. "You won." I motioned to Zeke. "Why don't you fellas play the next round? Just you two. I'll take winner." Zeke wanted nothing to do with the idea: What did I think he was, nuts?

In the silence I heard Gwynn's deep voice. "In the room the women come—" but the new guy cut him off with a fierce look.

"Shut up," he said. He turned back to me. His bitter lips demanded an explanation. Tremors of loathing rippled through his powerful body. His fists were red and white clumps of fury. I realized there was no place for me to shelter. I was fortune's plaything. I was toast on a stick. Curiously enough, however, I felt a smile surfacing through the stiff flesh of my face.

From what seemed far away I heard Gwynn mumble to himself, "Oh, shit, oh, shit, I should have been a pair of ragged claws." Then, without moving, the new guy let loose with this caterwaul. For a moment I thought it was the heating system screeching to life. It seemed to emanate from the eight corners of the big room. The onlookers began shuffling behind me for protection as the new guy brought the cue straight down on the table with a force that neatly snapped the stick into pieces, which scattered away from him across the floor. He held the jagged end up to my face. My mind was writhing like a nipped weasel. Even so, I felt I should speak. I felt I should say something on behalf of the rational world. But the one thing I knew I should not do became the very thing that presented itself to me with all the inevitability of death's darkness:

"Co co rico," I said slowly, my heart pounding.

Gwynn began to cackle.

"Co co rico," I repeated.

Before I could fully get my point across, the director had taken the new guy into her arms, where he collapsed, weeping softly. She was a mother. She was all mothers. Tufted, enraged, she stared at me with bitter eyes as she caressed the back of his neck, the place where his beautiful hair met the vulnerable stretch of bone bridging his troubled mind with the rest of him.

Cellular

I'M FRANK LECUYER, seventy-two years old and descended
from French kings of the Middle Ages. But that was a long
time ago. Nowadays, I live with my wife, Gladys, who's been
mentally impaired for fifteen years. I'm used to it, but I don't
know if she's used to it because we haven't had a meaningful
discussion on that or any other topic for about fifteen years. I'm
not bitter about this, but it's not something I recommend, living in this manner. Then again, what choice do I have? I try
to keep things status quo. Household order helps, so does clar-
ity of intent. Things go back where they belong, the way she
would want them. We do talk. I often say something witty, and
she replies when it's appropriate—somehow she's still got the
timing down—so that if you were driving by our house or
walking dully along and looked in through the kitchen window
from the weeds past the edge of our yard and you overheard either of us in one of these moments, you might think we were
holding a conversation. You'd be wrong. When I talk to her, it's
exactly as though I'm talking to myself. There's no getting
around that fact. I've had time to think about this. I'm not

going to get technical about her condition. It doesn't affect her physical well-being, only her mind. She could live another twenty years. They call it something, but I refuse to attach a name to it. I've put any bitterness behind me. I'm not one to look skyward and ask, Why me? Because Frank Lecuyer harbors no illusions about whether an answer would be forthcoming. Why pose such a question?

Anyway, on an evening in late April, I'm standing at the kitchen window, the one that overlooks our small yard, beyond which runs a sloping meadow of weeds and wildflowers—the demesne of my idylls, humble as they are. The sun hangs over a distant ridge called Sleeping Giant, named for its resemblance to the profile of a big guy lying down. Gladys has finished working her way through the evening meal. It is just past six o'clock. I am washing her dinnerware, a set of brightly colored plastic trays and utensils, cerise and Day-Glo orange saucers—I don't know why I've kept them all these years—when I see something that makes me stop short, suds crawling down my forearms. Two gentlemen are walking up the slope from a large parked sedan—looks like a new black Lincoln, a jellybean like all the other models—toward the center of my meadow. Let me be clear on this point: I don't literally own the meadow.

"Gladys," I say, "look at that."

"Circus," she says, or at least that's what it sounds like. I've spent years divining these utterances. Conclusion: They're undivinable. They're inscrutable. And that's fine. Some say there's providence in the fall of a sparrow. I don't. End of discussion.

"Two men," I say. "Out there in the field."

She laughs food into her hands.

"Calm yourself, Gladys."

I dry my palms on my apron, step to the sliding door, and whistle for Tex, my elderly whippet, who is up the cellar stairs and at my side in a moment. "What do you make of that?" I ask him. He looks up at me with a quizzical expression.

"Lift me," he says. "I can't see what you're referring to."

I'm so intrigued by the situation evolving out there in the sunlight that I don't say anything about his having ended a sentence with a preposition. Instead, I pick Tex up and carry him onto the deck.

"Two men," he says. "How curious."

I don't like the look of things, and I tell him as much, standing on the outer edge of my property now.

"You tend to put the worst face on a situation," he says. Then he glances back over my shoulder at the open sliding doors.

"Don't worry about Gladys," I say. "She'll be OK for a minute without me."

"Tell me. Is there a word for the phobia that someone can read your mind?"

I ignore him. One of the men spots us and waves a hammer. Tex jumps down. "Don't say a word," I tell him. "Let me do the talking."

"I know the drill," he says sadly.

"Hello," one of the men says, a black man, his hand out. He seems friendly. The other man is a white guy, short, somewhat fierce-eyed. He stays back a way. He's holding signage in his hands. "Whoa, that looks like a little greyhound." He crouches to greet Tex. "Look at this. What is this? Is this a little greyhound?"

"Whippet," I say. "Can I help you?" I really want to tell them to get the hell out of the field, but I still subscribe to a loose set of customs and mores that requires at least a perfunctory nod toward hospitality. Tex growls and sniffs. He's always been particularly adept at making noises like these, though sometimes he overdoes it.

"You live there?" The white man asks as he pats Tex's ribs. Tex gives me a quick glance over his lean shoulder, eye cocked.

"Yes," I say. "Right there."

The black man speaks: "I don't know if you know yet, but right over *there*"—he points to the middle of the meadow—"is where there's going to be a cellular phone tower."

I'm speechless. Nor is there any expression in Tex's face. "Say what?" I manage.

"A transmitter. Didn't you know?"

Tex and I shake our heads at the same time. I confess that I can go for weeks without reading the local paper, there being many other uses for newsprint.

"Well, see that?" he says, motioning to his partner, who holds up the sign in response. "That's the announcement. That's the official public notice. We're legally bound to provide public notice. We're talking couple of months, maybe a month, and we're looking at a cell tower right there." The man points again.

"Come here, Tex," I say. Tex slinks over to me. Then to the men: "This is the first I've heard of it."

"Right," the white guy says. "Not a big one, though. There's plenty bigger than this one'll be."

"How big?" asks Tex.

"Buck twenty," he answers, without noticing who's spoken. The black guy looks a little nonplussed. He's wondering if he heard correctly. He's wondering, Did that dog just say something?

I barely notice. It's all happening at once. My chest is flooded with regret. My heart aches, and a drowsy numbness dulls my sight. I manage to reach down and lift Tex by the loose skin of his neck. My heart's pounding in my ears. Goddamn it, I think, we should have bought the meadow back in the day. They don't let big pieces of land lie open like that, not forever, not the powers that be. But it was as though we already owned it. For a time, I even passed the mower over it once or twice a week. I remember running Tex out here the first time we saw our property, the year after I retired from the post office, back even before we decided to buy. I mentioned it to him then — buying a bigger parcel — and he laughed it off. I remember his flippant demeanor. He was right: Gladys and I couldn't afford it. He was always right!

"A cell tower," I stammer. "But my panorama, look," I bid them to gaze with my arm, an almost royal gesture. "It's the whole reason we bought in the first place, twenty years ago, the sweeping view of the Giant. Won't it obstruct my view, this, this tower?" My tongue feels coated with ash.

"Obstruct?" the black man says. "No, no, no. It's just a pole, sir, with a triangular strut and some semicylinder-looking things at the top. There'll be no obstruction. You won't even notice it. No, uh-uh. *Obstruction* is a poor choice of words for what's going to happen here."

It's too much for me. I'll have no more of it! Away! Away!

"Let's go, Tex," I mutter finally.

Back on the deck, I watch the men pound the post for the public notice sign. Something is melting. Something is moving inside me. The panic is morphing into something else. I picture myself sitting out on the patio with the shadow of the cellular tower falling on me in the late afternoon. I might as well live out on the interstate. I might as well live in the middle of an antenna farm.

My idylls. All I can think of is my idylls.

"This will not stand," I whisper to myself, finally. Through the sliding glass doors I see Gladys smiling in my direction.

Tex lifts his ears. "What's that you said?"

"Nothing. I'm just weighing my next move."

"Your next move? Do you have a next move? Are you suggesting some kind of lawsuit, Frank, to block the construction of the tower? I mean, these cellular telephone companies have deep pockets, they're fully capitalized, and you're living on a fixed income. You're a retired postman, Frank. You're cash poor. Unless you've been hiding something from me all these years. A Swiss bank account? What could your next move possibly be? What lawyer would take on something like this, a cause so utterly futile? Next move, indeed, Frank."

I slump into my plastic patio chair as he prattles on. "You know, Tex, you can be a real depressing son of a bitch sometimes." We lock eyes. A breeze stirs the short hairs on his ears. Time passes. We're waiting for each other to speak. I'm conscious of birds calling from the meadow. Finally, he crunches up his thin lips and lays his head down on his side. "I heard that comment back there in the meadow," I say. "Have you forgotten our agreement?"

"No, I haven't," he mumbles.

"I love you, Tex, but you do remember our agreement, don't you?"

"I won't let it happen again," he says.

"I don't need to be worrying about our agreement, Tex, not on top of everything else."

"Frank," he says, "I assure you it won't happen again."

"And how can I be certain of this?"

"Because," he says, "I give you my word as a gentleman."

We're quiet for a long moment. I assume the issue is settled, and then he says, without looking up, "Frank, am I the only one who knows about the mail?"

"The what?" I say. "Shut your mouth." He's wearing this smirk. I won't have it.

"It's just a harmless question," he says.

"Shut!"

"Here's another one: How long has it been down there?"

"Drop it, Tex." He knows he's playing with fire. I'm not going to take abuse from a dog. But that accursed mail. It's my albatross. Tex has never brought it up before, nor have I thought of it myself for years. Though I've never gotten rid of it, have I? Five black plastic contractor's bags crammed full of mail, down in the cellar. What is there to say? It was a bad time in postal history. I was delivering other carriers' day-end overload. The newspapers were full of stories about incompetence in the upper ranks. Things were getting out of hand. For a month or so, I brought my own daily overload home. Not standard operating procedure, I know. My plan was to remail it slowly, in the fullness of time, but it's too late now. What I have in my basement is a load of dead letters. But have I even as much as opened a single one of them? Never. There could be cash in some of those envelopes, but I can't bring myself to look for it. "You know how long it's been there," I say to Tex. "It's a dead issue now. In the grand scheme, it's no big deal."

"Really, Frank?" Tex grins. "No big deal? A federal crime is no big deal?"

"Drop it," I say. I watch cloud shadows slide across Sleeping Giant. "Now lick my hand like a proper whippet and that'll be the end of it."

At times I need to remind him of his place in the order of things, but it never sits well with him. I would not use words like *master* or anything so crude, but he's a dog and I'm his *owner*, though that's another word I'm hesitant to employ. Tex is not amused. He won't look at me. And not wanting to make anything more of the matter, I let sleeping dogs lie.

Over the course of the next two months I watch from my kitchen window, and from my bathroom window, and from the patio with rum and Coke in hand while Gladys takes the evening breeze with me and Tex, and from the seat of my lawn mower—the leaves of grass blown like chaff from wheat in the rough winds of early summer—as the tower begins to take shape. Its triangular steel struts climb higher, mocking me, and crows balance on the guy wires like the black stain of cancer in the cool of the morning.

I mark July 3 as the day I finally come to terms with my destiny, the moment fate sticks its nose under the tent of inevitability and I realize the purpose of my life, or what's left of it. Gladys is asleep in our room—her afternoon nap. And Tex? What does Tex say when I reveal my world-shaking plan? We are standing in the driveway next to my yellow Cadillac. Water runs in black rivulets down the length of the sloped tarmac and into the street, pooling there like mercury and mirroring a featureless summer sky. Tex laps at a muddy puddle. "I'll get a bowl if you're that thirsty," I say.

"Don't bother," he says. "I don't want to put you out."

"No, really. It's no bother." I hear Gladys snoring through the open bedroom window. "Tex?" I say.

Tex looks around as though confused. "Yes?"

"Tex, I'm going to say something, and I don't want you to repeat it."

"Sure," he says. "Shoot."

I pause, letting the drama build. "I think I'm going to have to take down the tower."

The only part of Tex that moves is his eyes — left, right, then back at me. "Take down the tower," he says flatly.

I turn off the hose and watch the water bead on the Caddy's hood. I'm trying to act nonchalant.

"Wait." Tex moves closer. He's not even panting anymore. "Take down the tower? Did you say take down the tower? Tell me you didn't say what I think I heard you say."

Two crows pass overhead, their dense shadows running quickly over Tex, up the driveway, and past me. "You heard correctly."

"Wait," he says. "How? When?"

"When it's completed," I say. "For maximum effect."

"For maximum effect." He pauses. "Is that a wise choice? I mean, taking down the tower?"

"No," I say. I'm enjoying this. "It's probably not a wise choice."

"What if you get caught?"

"It's a matter of *when* I get caught. Not *if*."

Tex takes a deep breath. "Frank, I hope what I'm about to say doesn't strike you as self-centered. You know me. But if you go away, like, to the big house or whatever you want to call it . . ."

I'm nodding. "Probably a federal prison facility. It's practically an act of terrorism, what I'm planning."

Tex swallows. I've never seen his brow so furrowed. I'm struck by how old he's getting. "Right," he says. "So what happens to me? I'm in no shape to be fending for myself. I'm no spring chicken, so to speak. I wouldn't last thirty-six hours out in the wilderness."

I look down at my shoes. "I hadn't really thought that through, but you do have a point. Gladys would finally be institutionalized. She'd be taken care of. No question about that. There would be time to see to the details. It's been coming a long while now, anyway. But you, Tex? I'd have to be more inventive. I could give you to that new family on Muncie Street."

"Not the house with the ducks?"

I'm nodding again. "You don't sound too thrilled."

"Can I be Frank?" Tex says. It's the beginning of one of our longest-running jokes. But when I deliver the comeback — "No, *I'm* Frank" — he doesn't even fake a smile.

"I *like* what we have right here," he says. "We have it good. Hell, *you* have it good. Gladys loves you. You have a great house, on a great piece of land. You're retired. Why throw it away?"

Just then Gladys awakens and begins to scream. There's no need to rush. It's never an emergency, just the flooding realization she experiences when she opens her eyes and confirms once again that she's still in the world. Still part and parcel of this realm of desire and defeat. Or at least that's how I read it.

"Your anxiety has been duly noted," I say, leaving Tex standing at the end of the drive.

During the week between my revelation to Tex and the day the tower is completed — the day the crane that hoisted the cellular hardware to the turrets folds down onto itself and rumbles into the distance — my whippet and I hardly speak. In the mornings, the unrisen sun sets the tower's highest struts gleaming in pinks and lavenders. But the beauty only adds to my sense of loss. It's as though the tower has always been there. Sometimes I'm in the mood to talk, but Tex is unusually petulant and morose. Then when he finally comes around, I really don't want anything to do with him.

Later, I leave him home when I take Gladys to Home Depot with me. There I buy a blowtorch and the heaviest power drill I can find, holding each tool up for her inspection. She nods and sometimes even handles the hardware herself. I buy a hacksaw and some blades. I buy a pair of tongs with thick rubber insulation on the handles, a small sledgehammer, a welder's helmet and mitts, and one of those heavy aluminum flashlights. I buy bolt cutters.

The moon is full that weekend, so I push Judgment Day back another fortnight. I need darkness. I've tested the strength and tension of the guy wires on brief daylight reconnaissance trips into the meadow. I think I know which wires need to be severed, and which heads of which securing bolts need to be superheated and twisted away. From there on in, it's simply a matter of patience: I'm aware, roughly, of how long it will take to cut through the leg of the west-facing lower strut. I must begin soon after dark, but early enough to do the entire job in a single night. It's a one-timer. It's all or nothing.

Sunday, July 14. Bastille Day.

The daylight hours pass uneventfully: I feed Gladys. I bathe Gladys. She seems a little wary. I catch her staring at me more than once, and I'm almost convinced she knows that something untoward is afoot. We sit on the patio in the shadow of the ranch, and I read aloud from the arts section of the Sunday newspaper—an article on contemporary sculpture, a retrospective of the photographs of William Wegman. I hold up a shot of three of those dogs of his, arranged to form the letter A. Gladys listens intently, nodding sometimes, her forehead creased as in days of old. A little later, I notice she's been asleep for some time. I permit myself just one glance at the cell tower. Two crows hulk on the edge of one of the antennas against a sky boiling with cumulus clouds. I imagine the thousand signals finding their way to the tower receivers, thousands more emanating from its conical transmitters—people whispering erotic things to one another over the airwaves, people crying, cursing, delivering horrific news. Somewhere there's a man in his late forties, drunk as he speeds along the interstate, frazzled, unshaven, his life in ruins. He's finding it difficult to keep between the white lines of his lane. He's dialing the number of some lost love with one hand, listening to the ringing on the other line, listening, waiting for this woman to pick up, wondering if he's got the right number or whether he'll even know what to say if she does.

"Tonight's the night," I whisper to Tex. He's lying in a lithe semicircle of whippet, his ribs rising and falling, asleep himself. Gladys hasn't made a noise for hours, dozing upright. So I lift and carry her to the bedroom—amazed at my own strength—and undress her and put her nightgown on her, and carry a small tray to the bedside and brush her teeth and wipe her lips and finally lower her back on the bed. Then I lie with her, my clothes still on, and wait for night to fall. For a long time, even before her illness, I used to watch TV until well after midnight, all the talk shows, the news, then shuffle in and collapse next to her. It didn't dawn on me that this seemingly insignificant habit, over time, was eroding our life together. Gradually, I've returned to the ceremonies of that former life—it seems so long ago—primary among which was that of climbing into bed together for the night and waiting for sleep to take us both.

As I lie listening to Gladys breathe, I descend into that state between sleeping and wakefulness. The words *Bastille Day* drift in and out of my consciousness. I'm thinking about guys with muskets and wine-stained lips; people dressed in motley with strange, shapeless hats; a crowd singing the French national anthem; all of it in black and white. Then—it seems only a moment later—I'm fully awake and fumbling my new tools into a duffel bag. In the kitchen, I whistle softly for Tex. Nothing happens. I whistle again, and he slinks up the basement stairs and stands waiting for me at the sliding doors to the patio. I put my finger to my lips.

"We have to keep it down," I say.

"You're really going through with this."

I just nod and snap my new flashlight on and off.

"Frank, is there anything I can say or do to convince you to put away this folly?" he asks, his whippet face dour, tail motionless.

I look at Tex. At first, I decide I'm not going to say anything, but then it all comes tumbling out. I unload: "For God's sake, Tex, something has to change around here. Haven't you noticed? The days are just passing one after another. It's all so formless and indistinct anymore. The cycle seems unbreakable. It's just . . ." I pause. "The snow is about to slip from the bamboo leaf."

He's looking at me with a squint.

I continue. "It feels right, deep inside somewhere. You should know about these things. You're closer to the natural order than I am, the circadian rhythms."

"Excuse me?"

"Anyway, I think I can get away with it. How the hell are they going to know it was me? I was entirely too hasty in assuming the trail would lead back here. That was hubris talking. Who am I? No one's going to remember that encounter in the meadow." I take a breath. "Tex, it's all about potential energy. Someone's got to release it. Great chains of events sometimes begin with a single simple action. Who knows why the snow slips suddenly from the bamboo leaf?"

Now Tex is shaking his head. "Frank, what the hell are you talking about? Are you for real? It's July. What snow?"

I snap off the yard lights, then step off the patio and into the cool black air. "I refuse to get into a discussion of rhetorical figures with you, Tex. I know you know what a metaphor is." Tex lags behind me for a short distance, then stops in the middle of the wet grass. "Suffice it to say: somehow, the moment I knew this tower was going up, I knew I'd be taking it down. Haven't you ever known something viscerally like that before, known it on some deeper level before consciously knowing it? You're a dog, for Pete's sake."

Tex barks a short sharp canine syllable. I'm taken aback by its volume. The sound races past me into the distance, then races back as a faint echo from beyond the meadow, as though originating from within the dark hollows of Sleeping Giant itself.

"Keep it down," I say. I'm serious now. Tex follows me just a little distance more, to the edge of the yard.

"Stop right there, Frank," he says. There's something in his voice that I've never heard in all our years together, something deep and ancient. He's almost growling now. "Don't make me do this."

"Do what?" I ask, but I think I know what he's suggesting. I can barely see him back there in the darkness. He's like a shadow, a silhouette, nothing more.

"I can make one hell of a racket, you know. I can run up and down the block and have all the neighbors out on their lawns in no time."

Not likely, I'm thinking. Whippets are a high-strung but essentially quiet breed, vulnerable to cold and to fractures of their shockingly spindly lower legs and ankles.

"You've been good to me, Tex." I'm talking into the darkness now, my back to him, and I can trace the latticed outline of the cell tower against a black metallic sky. Then I start walking away again; I force myself to.

"Frank," he calls out hoarsely. "Frank." His voice gets louder: "Frank! Don't do it. Stop, Frank!" I look back to see him leap straight into the air. He's illuminated for a moment in a slant of stray light, then drops back into the darkness. It's the last I see of Tex. I'm walking now. I don't look back again. I just keep walking away, stepping into the high grass of the meadow. I don't slow down. "Frank!" he yells again and again. "Frank!" But each iteration seems more and more like an animal noise, until I can no longer distinguish the sound of my name from the unmistakable sound of a dog in pain somewhere behind me in the night.

Rear View

I DRINK NINE AND A HALF glasses of Chardonnay in the bar at the Hyatt. Now I'm behind the wheel of my brother-in-law's new Nissan Pathfinder. He did not feel well enough to drive, but I think he is out of the woods now. I can hear him breathing in the passenger seat. Near a building in Denver with zebra stripes and no windows, I pull up to the curb, lost. The building is a strip club. It is two o'clock in the morning, and the place is emptying out. Nearby, the door of an idling charter bus welcomes dazed patrons. Three people are staring at me—two men, and a woman between them who, I think, is smiling. She walks over to the Nissan Pathfinder. Can we give them a ride downtown? she asks. Keeping her face in my field of vision is a challenge, like talking to a balloon in a stiff breeze. I ask her where Pete's Kitchen is. "Pete's Kitchen?" she says. She seems relieved. "Shit, that's right on the way." I turn to my brother-in-law. I see him once, sometimes twice a year if the year includes a wedding, like tomorrow. We live in different states. He is a lawyer. I am not. We are married to sisters. He confided in me an hour ago at the Hyatt over a game of nine ball that he has never masturbated, not once in his life. I asked him if he was serious. He told me he was. I had to believe him. I told him I could not keep my hands off myself.

He says to let the three people in. I say, "Get in." The three people get in.

My brother-in-law and I are still what some people might refer to as young men. But those people are fewer and fewer, and once my brother-in-law told me he hoped he had not already fallen prey to a form of *insidious domestication*. He used those very words, his eyes a little moist. Lawyers are precise in their diction. That was another late night. We had played Scrabble for six hours. It was Christmas Eve. Our in-laws were asleep. A blizzard was dropping three feet of snow, and then we found ourselves on the way to the riverboat casino in Rock Island, Illinois, where we would lose several hundred dollars on blackjack and my brother-in-law's eyes would grow moister still. But maybe it was only *accommodation,* he was saying, maybe just a *temporary accommodation.* "Jesus!" he wailed. "I made wheat bread last weekend, in one of those white appliances!" But the way in which he tells me to tell these three people to get into his new Nissan Pathfinder tonight is his way of letting me know he knows I know we are really at core still open, *radically* so, to whatever raw contingency crass hap is apt to dish up. Tonight we are not mortgage holders. We are not fathers. Stretching before us is not a life spent on the telephone in beige-carpeted offices during the cool of the day. Tonight we are noir heroes. We are drifter existentialists.

The people slide into the back seat, and I pull away from the curb. The Pathfinder shows 2,532 miles. It is the newest vehicle I have ever driven. It's loaded—leather throughout, tinted windows, heated seats. The man sitting behind me leans forward. He has his arm around the woman's neck. "Yo," he says, "I own these."

It is not immediately apparent what the man means, though there is nothing subtle about his breath, which smells of peppermint schnapps and jalapeños.

He says, "These are my titties." Behind us the man begins

pinching the woman's breasts with both hands and jimmying his stubbled chin into the crevices of her neck. She writhes and slaps at his hands. I can see it all in the rearview.

My brother-in-law looks at me. I look at my brother-in-law. He keeps what hair he has left close-cropped, the top of his head sunburned and shiny.

"I made twenty bucks a pop tonight dealing sneak peeks at these titties," the man says. "Over four hundred bucks." He reaches into his breast pocket. "See this?" he says, holding a roll of bills with a thick elastic band around it up to the light.

The man on the other side of the woman slurps drool back into his mouth. "Get your sneak peeks at these sweet teats," he says. He may have an accent or he may have a speech impediment. We glide past a closed-out Caldor's and a weedy lot with an overflowing dumpster. Stray greyhounds stand around chomping garbage. The mountains are invisible somewhere. My wife sleeps in a king-size bed back at the Hyatt. She is drifting away from me, toward dawn.

"Where are you boys from?" the woman asks. The complex glare from store windows and the street lamps moving over us play hide-and-seek with her facial features. I try to concentrate. All I can tell is she has blond hair.

"He's from Iowa," I say.

"There's nothing there," says the guy with the accent. "'Cept a fuckload of corn." He is shaking his head and laughing through his nose.

"Sure," I say. "He's an officer of the corn."

Silence.

"Fucking stupid," says the titty purveyor.

The woman leans forward with her hands on the headrests. "What's your names?"

"I'm Bob and he's Jim," my brother-in-law says. It is a lie.

"Oh, fuck you guys," the woman says. "You're so full of shit."

I look at my brother-in-law. He is recovering from a cringe, his eyes round and worried, his shoulders slumped. He refuses to look at me. Everything about him asks, What have we done?

"You fucking liars," she says.

We stop at a red light. A 1965 Cadillac traverses the intersection in front of us, hubcaps, whitewalls, windshield, and chromework adazzle.

"That's piss-poor," she says. "You can't lie any better than that?"

"They're common enough names," I say.

"Yo." The titty proprietor leans forward. "Yo. You guys interested in seeing these titties?"

I wait as long as I can, eyes forward. Then I speak. I speak for myself and I speak for my brother-in-law, this superlative attorney who has never masturbated. "No," I say as I angle the Pathfinder onto the main thoroughfare. "That's all right." I am trying not to seem in a hurry. "Yo," I say. The street is almost completely void of traffic now. "We're cool."

The woman laughs. "You guys ain't cool, let me tell you that right off."

There is a short silence into which the drooling guy snickers. "Whaddaya make of these fucking guys?" he says, slapping the back of my brother-in-law's seat.

"No, but really," says the titty purveyor. "You want to see them?"

I look into the mirror. "We're all set," I say, cranking as much gratitude as possible into my tone. "We're doing just fine," I say.

"For free," he says. "In exchange for your refreshing hospitality."

The woman hears what is playing on the radio. "Hey, Jim," she says, "turn this shit up."

I turn it up.

"No, louder," she says.

I turn it up louder. Chaka Khan's voice floods the Pathfinder. "Tell Me Something Good." In eerie falsetto, the woman behind me sings along:

> Your problem is you ain't been loved like you should.
> What I got to give will sure 'nough do you good.

The drooler is playing air bass as the purveyor pounds the door handle to the beat. The two men are breathing in and out, in and out, fast, like Chaka's backup singers, a breathy chorus.

"Jesus, that's good," the purveyor says. "But no, really, I want to treat you guys." In the rearview mirror his head is haloed, his uncombed hair glistening in the white headlights of a following car. I do not say anything.

"Don't go making me mad by refusing my generosity like that, Jim. Hey, Bob? Come on, are you telling me you don't think she's fine? I mean, look at her."

The woman preens, her lips in an exaggerated pout.

I look at my brother-in-law. He does not look at me. I have never been to Denver before.

"I can't believe this. I'm offering you a twenty-dollar free gift right now—forty, really, when you think about it—and you're snubbing me? It's like you're saying, Fuck you. Help me understand something here. Are you guys for real?"

The drooler hacks up some phlegm. He rolls down his window, spits into the breeze. Most of it blows back on him. He rolls the window back up. "Fucking Jimmy and fucking Bobby," he says. "Imagine the ingratitude."

I am not sure what to say, so I say, "We would take you up on the offer, but we're married."

The back seat of the Pathfinder explodes with laughter. "You're married?" says the woman. "Is that right? We're married, too, me and him—not to each other." Her eyes glow in a bright rectangle of reflected light. She has her arm around the administrator of her womanly trust. "We're all married," she says. "Everybody's married. See this asshole here?" She slaps the drooling man with the back of her hand. He snickers. "He's married, too—you should meet his wife. Don't be thinking saying you're married is like some magic wand you can wave at us to stop us from busting your balls."

"Sure, all right," I say. I do my best to chuckle. I nod my head. "I do hear what you're saying." Faint waves of nausea have been lapping at me for some time. It must be the wine. I realize a need for air. The fact is that we are a mile up. I roll my window down and begin to swallow mouthfuls of humid air.

"What's the matter, Jim?" the woman asks. "You don't look well."

"Look, I'm going to ask you fuckers one more time," the purveyor says. He takes a deep breath. "You want to see my titties here or not?"

I wait. Then I wait some more. I wait another second. It has begun to rain. Everyone is quiet. Then I speak. "Well, you talked me into it," I say. I'm shivering now. "All right, let's see what you got."

"Show time," he says, rubbing his hands together. I watch in the rearview as the purveyor reaches behind to unhook her bra. I watch the woman settle herself in the seat, toss her hair, and lift her shirt up to her chin, a white Nirvana concert T, and there they are, what the hoopla has been about: her small bare breasts strobed by passing street lamps, her nipples gray-green in the strained light.

"*Look* at that," says the purveyor. He is sincere. "Just *look* at that."

I feel nothing. I'm empty.

"Hey, Bob?" he says. "So what do you think?" My brother-in-law's damp forehead is pressed to the Pathfinder's passenger-side window. He has shut his eyes. His neck is sunburned and wet. In the light, an artery there is jumping to the rhythm of his heart. "Bob," says the titty purveyor, "I'm not going to ask you again, Bob. You don't know what you're missing. Hey, asshole, the world is passing you by."

Scissors

for Paul Soucy

I WAS SITTING in Renny St. Cyr's barbershop, looking out at the textile mills across the highway and the big clock without hands. I hadn't been home to New Bedford in years. But I was out of work. My wife had left me. I had no savings, and at the age of thirty-one no choice but to move in with my mother until — her words — "something turned up."

When I came into the shop, Renny had nodded without expression. My mother had told me about Renny's cancer — she'd heard it from my uncle — but it was hard for me to believe he was sick. Renny looked the same as he always had. A thin man in his middle fifties, he still wore the black pompadour of his high school years, the same colorless straight-legged chinos, the neat short-sleeved cotton smock, mint green, that hung outside his pants like a bowling shirt. The same high-gloss patent-leather shoes.

The shop was tight, little more than a storefront that grew darker as you moved in, the way a cave does. There was only one barber chair. A round spot remained on the linoleum where its twin had long ago been torn out. Two huge green-tinted mirrors hung on opposing walls. On a short shelf below the chair mirror stood a couple of cardboard displays for "Unbreakable Combs" —a cartoon strongman bending one of them between his meaty fists—and flattop "Krew Wax." Along the wall opposite the cutting chair, we customers waited in green and chrome seats with plastic armrests. There were a few old-timers in loose-fitting shirt-jacs and two or three younger guys in blue dickeys and work boots. A couple of men, on break from the Our Bread Baking Company just up Purchase Street, wore white pants and grimy T-shirts. Above us, a ceiling fan spun slowly.

I started flipping through an old issue of *Popular Mechanics*. I read a few paragraphs on homemade helicopters. Gyro-copters, they're called. You build them from spare lawn mower parts, lift off right from your driveway, and commute to work by air. Another article featured diagrams of the Stealth Bomber's landing gear. There was a dramatic photo of the black aircraft silhouetted against a yellow moon. Then I remembered that today was the day of the solar eclipse. There hadn't been one in North America in ten years, not since before I'd left home the first time.

I shot another glance at Renny. He looked all right to me, a little thinner maybe, older. He might have shaken it, I thought. My uncle had been wrong before. But then I noticed something. Every so often as he circled the chair while working on a customer, he shook out his legs, like an Olympic swimmer getting ready to enter the pool. I wasn't the only one to notice. After a while an old guy wearing a cowboy hat pointed and said, "Hey, Renny, you nervous about something?"

"What if I am?" Renny shot back in his deadpan voice.

"I'm just asking."

"I'm just telling," Renny said.

"I just thought you was nervous about something," the man said. "You look nervous."

Renny stopped cutting hair. He held the scissors above the

place he'd been working. Without the slightest movement in his face, he looked at the old guy. He kept looking until the man's eyes fluttered away.

"I was just asking," the man said again. The sunlight from the window behind him made the hair in his ears glow.

Renny kept looking, silently, until the room grew very uncomfortable. The radio played its music too softly to decipher. It might have been Bobby Darin's "Mack the Knife." No one said anything until the man in the hat stood up and, trailing a few feeble words about coming back when the wait got shorter, left. Renny followed him out the door with his eyes. Only after the small leather strip with the bells stopped jangling did he go back to cutting hair.

My throat felt like paper. I swallowed hard without moving my head. I knew Renny's attitude could be less than winning—when I first started coming into the shop I'd been the recipient of his cutting words—but here was something different. Staring at a diagram of hydraulics, I felt a need to fill the silence. The smell of hair tonic became unbearable.

"There's going to be an annular eclipse of the sun today," I said aloud, finally. Everyone looked at me except Renny, but no one said anything. Then he caught my eye in the mirror. I'd always thought Renny liked me—as much as he could like anyone.

"Annular," he said, trying out the word. "What's that?"

I'd been offered a window, fleeting and small. I wouldn't abuse the privilege. I knew where I was. "Moon's too far out to cover the whole sun," I said, my hands working. One was the moon, the other the sun. "So it makes a ring instead." The men returned to their newspapers.

"Yeah?" said Renny.

I went on. It was a million to one we happened to live on a planet whose moon and sun appeared roughly the same size in the sky. I mentioned the curious effect of horns peeking above the horizon when such an eclipse occurred close to sunrise or sunset.

"Horns. Interesting," Renny said, snapping on the electric shears. I'd had my say.

Fifteen minutes and two haircuts later a woman opened the door and came in. All heads rose except Renny's. She wore a filthy terry cloth outfit — powder blue shorts and tank top. Wrinkled, they didn't fit — too small and too big, sort of. The eddying dust slowed in the sunlight as she leaned against the wooden windowsill. No one offered her a seat. She took out a crushed box of Marlboros from the waistband of her shorts and the lighter she'd been carrying. As she lit up, I saw that her fingers were cracked and hardened. A fish cutter. Was she with one of the men? The others seemed to be thinking the same thing. Just as it became clear that she wasn't, Renny asked, "Can I help you with something?" He was sculpting an arc over a customer's ear, his scissors catching the light from the window.

"Haircut," she said hoarsely. She cleared her throat. A cigarette voice, I thought. Her dirty blond hair hung stringy and formless around her face.

"Excuse me?" asked Renny.

"I'm due for a cut." She had to push her voice out. The effort seemed to exhaust her.

"Nope. Not here."

The woman coughed a cloud of blue smoke. "Huh?"

"Not here you're not."

"What do you mean not here?"

"Not here," Renny said without looking up. Then: "Do I stutter?"

She put her hands on her hips. "Well, why the hell not?" The cigarette danced in her mouth.

"Simple. I don't do women's hair."

"Your father did."

There was a long pause, as though her last words would settle it. The floor snapped beneath Renny's shoe. He spoke slowly: "Before he died, my father hadn't cut hair for twenty years."

"He did so," the woman said, folding her arms. "I been in here."

Renny looked around the shop, then stood on his toes, peering into the back room—the kind of thing I'd seen him do before. Back then, it was a playful goofing on someone, and I'd smiled because I'd been in on the joke. I'd been one of the guys. But it was different now. I was thirty-one. I'd seen some things. I felt a little short of breath.

"You may not have noticed, but I'm not my father," he said.

The woman snorted. She unfolded her arms. "Hell with it then," she said. She threw the lit cigarette at a nest of hair on the floor and walked out, leaving the door ajar. One of the men, an old guy in a faded Hawaiian shirt, got up and closed it quietly, deliberately, then rubbed out the cigarette with his shoe, picked it up, and put it in the trash. He sat down, but then he got up again, picked up the wide push broom, and began sweeping the ash and the fallen hair into a pile in the corner. A faint scent of singed hair drifted through the room. The radio continued to play too softly to be heard.

As he sprinkled powder on a round-handled wooden brush, Renny said, to no one in particular, "Cut a woman's hair, you're looking for trouble." He was talking to the swirl at the top of the customer's head. "I'm not equipped for that," he said. He pulled down the back of the man's collar and brushed away the stray clippings.

The guy who'd cleaned up shifted in his seat. "Though she probably only wanted a buzz cut. You know, a butch cut."

Renny put down his scissors. "I have enough to deal with, with the men who come in here." He wasn't smiling. He shook out the apron as the customer he'd been working on stood up. He glanced at a man sitting against the back wall. One of Renny's talents had always been knowing, even in a crowded shop, who was next. The man got up.

"See her, though?" the old-timer continued. "Kind of manly."

"You think?" one of the men from the bakery said. Some of the other men laughed. I picked up another magazine and lowered my head. The air had taken on a sort of oiliness. I reminded myself to keep my mouth shut.

Renny kept quiet, too. An utter stillness seemed to have descended on him. I tried not to stare, but every line of his body had changed. He no longer moved his legs. As he bent to pick up his scissors, I could see the ridge of his spine through his shirt, and I knew right then that he hadn't shaken the cancer. I felt cold.

Years earlier I'd come into the shop eager to have my hair shorn artlessly away. Renny could do it. A beezer. Two dollars and fifty cents. It was July, the month after my high school graduation. I was trying to simplify my life. Not having to wash my hair, being able to pass a soaped cloth over my head and call it clean would save me time, though I wasn't sure what I was saving it for. I had a summer job with the town cutting grass in the cemeteries and on the median strips along Route 6. My future had yet to congeal into anything like a life. I was keeping my options open. I was waiting for a sign. Sitting in the chair, I'd listened to Renny's account of his first and only crew cut.

"My wife told me not to do it," he said. "It was just after we were married."

"She didn't like crew cuts?" I looked at myself in the green mirrors, wondering whether I should go through with it. My face seemed too big already.

"No," he said, grinning. "Neither did I."

I tried to picture the shape and texture of his bare head. It wasn't easy.

"But you did it," I said.

"I did it."

"Why'd you do it?"

He shook his head. "I was happy." He snapped out the apron. "Everything was fine," he said. "She shouldn't have told me not to."

Between customers, Renny walked over to the window and lowered the blinds halfway. Suddenly, a dozen yellow wafers of light spanned the wall of the barbershop. I almost jumped out of my seat. The eclipse had begun. In fact, we were well into it.

The sun's disk looked as though it were being eaten away by some smooth-toothed beast. I pointed. "Look—the eclipse!" I yelled.

Renny jumped in place.

"Jesus Christ, you trying to give me a heart attack?" said the Hawaiian shirt man. I stretched my arm even farther, pointing. "What the hell is with you?" he said.

"The eclipse I mentioned earlier?" I said.

"The what?"

"The annular eclipse," I said. "It's on." I began rambling again about eclipse folklore. Dolphins swimming backward, for instance. Birds settling into trees as though it were night. The information just tumbled out of me, and I was sure half of it was nonsense. Before long, the men, shaking their heads, had gone back to their newspapers again. I spoke on into the silence for a while; then I stopped. The fever had passed. But talking hadn't driven away what weighed on me, how Renny had changed before my eyes.

I finally got into the chair. Now I could see some of the men reflected in the mirror. Some scary new guys had come in at the tail end of my spiel. Fishermen just back from the Georges Bank, they were huge, slicked with two weeks' work. They had spread out into the shop, bringing with them the rotting smell of the sea and a feeling of unease. But from where I sat their surly expressions, their soggy cigars, seemed merely amusing to me. It was as it had always been when I was in the chair. I was safe. I'd gone to my share of unisex hair salons, with the sterile track lighting and the expense. I was looking forward to the full Renny St. Cyr experience—the burn that the straight-edged razor left around the ears, the cooling splash of tonic, Renny's fingers soothing the newly bare space. I was in Renny's care now. Come what may.

The new men struck up a loud conversation. "Quite a knowledgeable fellow there," one of them said, nodding toward me.

His grimy pant legs disappeared into huge yellow work boots. He hadn't shaved in a while, and his disheveled red hair met his beard.

Someone I couldn't see from where I sat spoke up. "A real whiz." He had a voice like an oversized cartoon character. Bluto, to be exact.

The fishermen seemed to grow bolder in Renny's silence. Green smoke rose from their cigars.

"He should win a science fair."

"What do you say? What kind of haircut would suit such a intelligent fellow?" asked the red-haired fisherman. His face wore an expression of exaggerated contemplation.

A new man spoke up. "He looks a little sweet."

"You think so?"

"Whyontcha give 'm a bowl cut?" someone snorted. "Like Caesar."

"Just darlin'."

"Yeah, use a bowl for a caesar salad. Leave the oil." A laugh ran through the circle of men.

Renny watched the men in the mirror as he combed out my hair into a shapeless, comic mass. The laughter tapered. I tried to maintain a look of ease, but my face seemed pouty and prepubescent in that slant of light. I heard the wobble of the ceiling fan.

Just as the red-haired fisherman motioned to speak again, Renny cut him off: "You got a problem with the clientele?" At first I thought he was talking to me, but before I could answer he went on: "You do, you can scram."

Scram. That such a word could still be spoken without irony filled me with wistful delight. A soft wind ran through the weeds in the lot across the street.

"Hey, Renny," said the fisherman, "you letting in sweets like that, I don't want to be here anyway." His friends laughed.

Renny motioned over his shoulder toward the door. "Then scram."

I had the sudden desire to up and kiss Renny right there. On the cheek. It would have been so easy.

"Ruin my reputation," the fisherman said.

Renny stopped working and turned to him. "Well, I wouldn't want to do that." He reached for his scissors and started cutting.

I closed my eyes as the hair began to fall. Half a minute passed.

"So?" Renny shrugged as he worked. "What are you waiting for?"

The fisherman snorted loudly. "I'm going in my own good time, that's what I'm waiting for."

"Excuse me?" said Renny. "I have to see you out?"

"I'll leave in my own good time."

Renny let the silence gather just long enough. "Now."

The man didn't move. "You gotta say the magic word." He was trying to be funny, trying to find a way out, his voice unsteady now. Renny stopped working on my hair. I opened my eyes. In the green mirror his face was white and stiff as paper. No one laughed this time. The music from the radio had drifted into an undulating static.

Something snapped in me. I'd had it. I wasn't going to sit there and take this guff. What was I, a wuss? I twirled the chair around with my toe and tried to tear the apron from my neck with a clean macho jerk. But Renny forced me back down without looking away from the guy. He took a deep breath. "I been cutting your goddamn hair, guys like you, for thirty years." I could see his heart working under the mint polyester.

"Guys like me?" the man said, tensing forward in his seat.

"Idiots, yeah." Renny nodded. "Guys like you."

"Oh, idiots, is it?" The man's beefy hands gripped the armrests.

"Listening to your bullshit."

"Oh, is that right?"

Reflected in the mirror, the neat row of sun disks shone up my pant leg and across my chest. There they were—the horns —an exaggerated crescent. I couldn't tell whether the peak of the eclipse had passed or was still to come. But I knew we'd all be dead before there was another one like it in North America. This was it.

"You don't hear so well?" asked Renny. The scissors clattered as they hit the floor. A murmur rippled among the other men. The fisherman stood up in his oversized boots. He was in his mid-thirties, ruggedly muscled from the harsh work of his trade, and twenty years younger than Renny. But Renny stood his ground. He wasn't dying of cancer. He was standing tall, his hands in two marbly fists. He and the fisherman inched closer to each other. Outside, the light had become silvery and dull, like pewter. It was just after noon, the mills clear in the distance.

The fisherman smiled. His shoulders fell. He was backing down. "Hey, Renny," he said finally, waving him off with disgust. "Go fu—" But before the man could finish his thought, Renny head-butted him with a quick staccato motion, like dotting an *i*. The man staggered back, stunned, his jaw fallen, his eyes wide. The sound of the blow—like water slapped with an open palm—lingered in the air with the cigar smoke. Blood slicked a trail from the fisherman's nose to his stubbled chin.

Then I saw something I'd never seen before: Renny laughing. He shook his head. A few strands of the black pompadour lilted almost prettily. Then his mouth burst open as though he were surfacing after a long underwater swim: "Goddamn," he said. "Goddamn." He was laughing. Renny St. Cyr was standing in the middle of his barbershop, laughing. Not a cruel laugh. It didn't gloat. Each syllable tumbled forth smooth and green. The other men laughed now, too. In the opposing mirrors the walls seemed to expand into the distance, doubling and tripling the scene, making the men gathered there look more numerous. We were suddenly a crowd, a laughing crowd. Even the red-haired fisherman grinned, blood gathering under his chin in a bright red driblet. I was breathless. My jaw ached. My eyes stung.

But in that moment of common laughter, Renny was suddenly not laughing. His smile had tightened into a grimace. He dropped his head. A ghastly wail rose from his throat. Our laughter tapered off. Suddenly, we were back in Renny St. Cyr's barbershop.

Every eye was on Renny, his bent head, his arms hanging loose at his sides. I wanted to put my hand on his bony shoulder, just rest it there. I was standing right behind him. We were about the same height. I could have done it, easily. I still wonder what it would have felt like. But instead I bent over and picked up Renny's scissors. They were lying next to his shiny shoes, in a pile of my own fallen hair. It was the least I could do.

Something Like Shame

TI JEAN opened up the drugstore, and at about eleven, people began arriving, taking their places at the counter, ordering coffee. Ten o'clock Mass at Sacred Heart had let out. Sitting hunched by their wives, the men wore beige overcoats and felt hats. Coffee steamed from wax paper cups and mingled with the smoke from nodding cigarettes. Kids whined for more soda, relieved now to be out from under the intense eyes of God, and strained their own eyes to glimpse the covers of girlie magazines tucked high in the rack against the back wall. The cash register's occasional bristle and bang interrupted the voices of women in gloves and small hats with white netting that hung down over the eyes. In the air lingered the smells of paraffin and tepid holy water, burnt and buttered toast.

There was an almost palpable remorse after church on Sundays in North Fairhaven, something as disappointing and simple as rain but always unspoken, a secret you kept with the shiny streets. All the week's air had escaped, and the day stretched bland as newsprint toward the evening meal.

Between pouring coffee and trips to the register, Ti Jean would smile and wipe the counter, his elbow pumping vigorously. He hid his illiteracy well, humorously, feigning short-sightedness, asking customers to point to the cigarettes they wanted or to read their own illegible handwriting. He was a short man who, though in his middle forties, still lived with his mother on the third story of a tenement, a slight man with the unmistakable Canuck expressions and silent gestures of the hands and shoulders, though usually he kept his arms folded, hugging his small frame. He flicked a cigarette lighter absently, while leaning back against the pegboard on the wall behind him on which hung cheap pipes and balsa wood airplanes in pieces and wrapped in cellophane. All day his smile would surface but then dissipate without warning. The lines on either side of his mouth would deepen slightly, and he'd pass his fingers back through his thick black hair as though trying to smooth the creases in his forehead.

Armand, the owner, who had come in late, had been watching Ti Jean all morning but hadn't said a word yet, just stood staring at Ti Jean silently with that tight-lipped, pissed-off look. And that was strange, because there was a lot to talk about, especially after last night with the Sox taking two over New York, and the last game of the series at one o'clock that afternoon. In the spring Ti Jean and Armand had been to a few games together, had taken the train out of New Bedford to South Station, the subway to Fenway Park. Sometimes Ti Jean hated to think about those trips — not the trip up there itself exactly, which he loved, or the shock of seeing the ball field, green and perfect in the midst of the city's hectic black and white. Armand had been too nice, Ti Jean thought, too goddamn nice for his own good. They weren't friends, were they? It was just that Ti Jean worked for Armand, and for not a ton of money either. Going on twenty-five years — never late, never drunk on the job. Ti Jean had always been good for business, too. Customers loved him, came in just to feel square and solid about someone who knew them by name, knew if they took milk or sugar in their coffee, or whether a *mémère* was sick. A lot of people came in to see Ti Jean, *just* Ti Jean, especially on Sundays after morning Mass.

Sometimes Armand had no patience. Not that he didn't talk to people, but beyond the weather, a question or two about the family, fishing, or the Sox, he just wouldn't take the time. He couldn't, really, not with people calling in for prescriptions. So when one of the women started off about her husband's piles, Armand would stand there for a moment looking constipated, then grunt and walk away, maybe coming back with a tube of ointment and leaving it with Ti Jean to give to her.

Armand was watching Ti Jean now from behind the prescription counter, his wire-rimmed glasses visible between two flasks of colored water. His white hair, fairly short and never combed, curved absurdly away from his forehead. He had the habit—had had it since he opened the place—of coming out to the soda fountain, taking a Coke glass from below the counter, pumping two squirts of cola syrup, and swigging it down with a grimace, as though it were whiskey. Straight cola syrup. No soda. This happened twenty-five, thirty times a day. Today, though, he hadn't been out once from behind the high counter at the back of the store where he counted pills and looked up the pharmaceutical records he kept in the wall behind him. He continued to watch Ti Jean, and Ti Jean couldn't look back at him.

It was nerve-racking. Ti Jean had lost track of what a customer was saying. He was running back over in his mind everything that had happened the week before, short scenes involving the register and receipts for electricity bills, the chance position of objects under and around the counter—scissors and masking tape, for instance. Maybe he was pushing his luck with this register thing. Maybe Armand knew somehow. He imagined what his mother would say if she had known: "Well, it's a little late for 'sorry,' now, Ti." But it's for you, Ma, he thought. What do I need the money for? It's all for you. The customer carried on and on in a faraway pigeon voice. Under and around, Ti Jean was thinking. It had been raining all morning, but for a moment the sun glinted on the chrome of a passing car. I see sunlight in rain, Ti Jean thought, and he wondered—

as he had done since he was ti Ti Jean — Is there a rainbow? The customer yanked a thumb at an empty coffee cup. And as Ti Jean put the pot back in its heated cradle, he caught Armand's gaze. Ti Jean slid his fists deep into his pockets, clamped his jaw down so tight his ears hurt.

Twenty-five years is a long time.

It was quarter to noon. Father Eugene passed by the window. A moment later he sat at the corner of the counter amid a small gust of polite banalities. His bald head glossed by the fluorescent ceiling light, the priest asked for a cup of coffee. "Any word on the vandals, Father?" someone said from down the counter. A month or so earlier someone had broken into the sacristy during the night, stomped the ciborium flat, thrown it through the rose window. The chalice had simply disappeared. Father Eugene, almost in tears before the parish the Sunday after, had held up the object of the vandalism for all to see. The ciborium had come down from Canada with the priests who set up Sacred Heart Parish in the mid-nineteenth century, a burnished and hallowed object around which there had grown a tradition, a community. But now it looked like a flattened beer can.

Everyone at the counter turned to the priest for the latest news. There was still something raw about him. But before he could answer, Armand appeared with a small white prescription bag and placed it on the counter in front of Eugene, who dipped his chin. Armand nodded pointedly and went back to the prescription counter, passing Ti Jean with a heavy glance. Ti Jean smiled into the air and tried to wiggle the tension from his jaw.

Father Eugene shook his head. He grinned without warmth. Then he put down his coffee cup. "I'm surprised by the anger," he said, looking at his hands. The people at the counter seemed to bend in toward him. "You don't expect that kind of thing."

"It's creeps, Father, is all," said Ti Jean. He hadn't gone to Mass in years, but seeing a priest downhearted like that made him imagine the world in ruins, the little pockets of goodness here and there all dried up.

"It's hard to imagine the anger," said the priest. Ti Jean gave a stiff grin and shook his head vaguely. "Anyway. How's your mother, Ti Jean?"

"August wasn't a good month at all." He took a damp rag from his back pocket and wiped the edge of the counter, straightened the sugar jar and the chrome napkin dispenser. "Thanks for coming by last week. She appreciates it. I appreciate it." Father Eugene waved his free hand as he raised the cup to sip. Ti Jean liked the man. He was the kind of priest you could tell things—like about the makeshift bar in the back room where the men used to come on Sunday mornings before the real bars opened, to smoke cigars, play the one-armed bandit, drink beer and whiskey out of a Florence flask while their wives talked among themselves out at the soda fountain. That had been over and done with for some time now, ever since someone let on to the state police about the gambling. It had given Armand a scare. One Monday two state troopers came in with their baggy pants and black straps, their broad-brimmed hats in their hands. Armand walked out from behind the prescription counter looking guilty as hell. They said they wanted to take a look in the back room, said rumors had it such and such. Armand's shoulders went slack. He looked at his shoes. They followed him, but the room was empty—no slot machine and not a drop of liquor in the place. Ti Jean had been in back, heard the cops' deep voices, heard their boots on the wooden floor of the hallway. He grabbed the bandit—it must have weighed seventy pounds—ran out the back door and down Deane Street. When Armand saw the place was clean, he acted dumb, shrugged his tight French Canadian shrug, his face returning to its normal sour expression. Father Eugene loved this story; he'd laughed Coca-Cola through his nose the first time he'd heard it.

At noon, Larry dropped by the pharmacy for a pack of cigarettes. Larry took odd jobs when the house painter he helped didn't need him. He lived across the street, two floors above the Seaview Lounge, in a dark two-room apartment. He was already drunk. You could tell because he hadn't changed his clothes since the day before. He wore the same stained overalls he painted in, the same hat—a baseball cap that he'd flattened by folding in the crown and sewing it along the edge. He wore it high on his head and tilted back like a woman's pillbox. He reminded Ti Jean of the cliché about house painters being alcoholics and oversexed on account of all the lonely housewives. Ti Jean thought of a story Larry had told him over liver and onions about a woman he'd picked up at the Seaview. It was late, and he must have been very drunk, but he drove her to his trailer home in the park just over the Acushnet line. That was all Larry remembered of that night, but in the morning, when he woke up beside this woman and she rolled over and smiled, she didn't have any teeth. Larry cringed a smile. "They were over on the night table. On my side. Dentures." He cringed again, the slack beneath his jaw drawing taut. "The woman was elderly." Ti Jean pictured the whole thing—the wan flesh, everything. He himself had never slept with a woman of any age.

"Wow," he said softly.

"I thought she felt a little funny the night before," said Larry, taking a drag. "I could remember that at least."

"Old enough—"

"Yeah, yeah, I know—to be my mother." Larry shook his head.

That night had stayed with Ti Jean, had kept its power to move in him something like shame. Whenever Larry came in now, Ti Jean felt they shared something shameful, an awareness of a world coiled mean-tight and waiting to go off in your face if things got too good. The world had only to catch its breath sometimes—then you heard its laugh, loud and shameless.

When Larry sat down at the counter, most of the other customers got up to leave, moving silently away, mumbling apologies, and rattling stools. Larry snorted. "What? Do I smell?" He spread his hands, his elbows anchoring his arms to the counter. "Father?" The priest folded his top lip into his bottom.

"No more than usual, Larry," he said into his coffee cup. Ti Jean leaned back against the pegboard and snickered moronically.

"About those stolen things, Father," Larry started but then

hesitated when he saw how quickly Father Eugene's smile disappeared. "I didn't mean to change the subject, but they found them. They pulled a couple kids out of a stolen car. Upside down. Thirteen, fourteen—not even old enough to drive. Off that sharp curve on Deer Island Road. Both of them dead." Larry seemed ashamed at having brought it up. But you could tell there was a little pleasure at being the center of attention, at saying things—true things—that could change the expression on people's faces. It was a lonely person's pleasure. "That curve—you end up in six feet of water if you're not watching where you're going. I heard it over the scanner about an hour ago. A cruiser noticed the wheels just above the surface. It's low tide this morning. The chalice—in the trunk along with that cross you were talking about." The match Larry held burned down to his fingers; he dropped it and shook his hand in slow-motion pantomime. The priest sat silently.

"Who were they?" Ti Jean asked.

"They don't know yet. Kids."

Ti Jean folded his arms. "From around here?"

"They think Fall River. Out joyriding in a stolen car."

Father Eugene took a sip of coffee. "How long had they been down there?"

"For some time. They don't know exactly."

"Whose car?"

Larry shook his head. "Unknown." He looked up at the clock as he flicked cigarette ash in his empty coffee cup. "They probably have the things at the police station, Father. Maybe you should give them a call."

Eugene nodded his head and pursed his lips around his knuckles.

"It wasn't their car, these kids?" he asked absently.

Larry shook his head again. "Unknown."

"Horrible."

It had started raining heavily, and during the pause in the conversation Ti Jean could hear the rain water drumming in the drainpipes. He sighed. He put his foot up on the shelf beneath the countertop and thought of a night when he was eighteen, the year he started working at the drugstore. He had gotten shamefully drunk with some of the other boys from his graduating class. On the way home, alone at the wheel of his father's station wagon, his head lolling against the window, he'd watched the nose of the car bob crazily along the side streets, up and over curbs, the headlights raking across the façades of houses, flaring into darkened rooms. He remembered how distant the world of obligation had felt that night, how the thrust of the revving engine had become a feathery power tickling his damp fingers on the wheel of his father's Ford.

But then Armand stood at his elbow. Armand gave Larry and Eugene a short blink of both eyes and looked down. They saw that he was shaking beneath his white smock.

"Ti Jean—in back." He walked away. Ti Jean looked at Larry and Father Eugene, who sat motionless. He began again to check over the week in his mind. He saw the register spring open, heard it slam shut with that hint of a bell somewhere inside. Not this past week, he thought, no. Or had he?

Ti Jean hesitated at the door to the back room. In the half-light, Armand's form stood out against the pull-out prescription records that made up the wall and dated back thirty-five years. He had turned off—or had forgotten to turn on—the light that hung bare-bulbed by its own cord from the pressed-tin ceiling. He was leaning on a stepladder. His short frame was bent over, and he seemed to be straining to see something in the dark corner. The only light came from the hall.

"Something wrong with the light?" Ti Jean asked. He reached into the dark room hesitantly, carefully, as though he were trying to keep his sleeve dry while reaching into a tank of water.

"Leave it off," Armand said. He sounded out of breath. Ti Jean let his arm drop heavily at his side.

"OK. Sure." He wondered if Armand could hear him over the roar of the rain on the roof.

"About two weeks ago—a week ago last Tuesday—I had

three men come in." Armand worked his dry mouth. "Ti Jean, I'm losing money now. I called them in. What could I do?" He kept his eyes toward the corner.

"About what, Armand?" Ti Jean's thoughts had splintered like the flecks in a Formica countertop. "Who came in?"

"Come on, Ti. They came in—anyone can hire these guys—one of them paid exact change. One guy bought a lighter. The other guy bought two typewriter ribbons. It's not the first time, because I had to be sure. I didn't want to believe it, Ti. How could I?"

The room smelled of strongly of VapoRub. "Last Tuesday," Ti Jean said.

"A week ago Tuesday, Ti Jean! What does it matter? They came in one right after the other—you couldn't have known ahead of time." Armand still hadn't looked up. "That's how they catch people taking money. Whenever you don't have to open the register for change. They keep track of exactly what they spend. Then whoever hires them can check what shows up on the register tape. Ti, it's their job."

"Let's see," Ti Jean said, pretending to count on his trembling fingers. "Let's figure this out."

"How long have you been doing this? Just tell me the truth. Do me that small favor." Armand's shoulders were as still as concrete, but he seemed to be fighting for air. "I checked the register tape, Ti. It's not a lot. But it adds up. Over time it does."

By now Ti Jean's eyes had adjusted to the darkness; he could see Armand had been weeping. He drew back into the hall and pressed his forehead against the sharp corner of the wooden door frame. The streets would be slick with rain on the way home.

"Just tell me the truth, Ti."

But Ti Jean never heard these words. He was stumbling along the hall, clumsy with panic, choking on a bitterness he could no longer keep down.

Pious Objects

Qui perd sa langue, perd sa foi.

FATHER GASTON had just finished morning Mass before a nearly empty church of nodding parishioners, five elderly people scattered among the pews. He had delivered his brief homily—a few sentences, nothing more—in a looping, lilting French Canadian accent. Now, as he crossed the parking lot between the chapel and the rectory, in that same tone he murmured a disorganized prayer, interspersed with a list of things he needed to do that day. It had rained all evening and most of the morning, and the damp air caught Gaston's breath and held it white and frozen for a moment as he moved along with his head bent. *Novembre,* he whispered.

A week earlier, on his seventy-fifth birthday, he'd received a card from a seminary friend with whom he'd lost touch. Inside was an obituary clipped from a Montreal newspaper. The last of their seminary teachers had died at the age of ninety-seven. It was an odd way to fill a birthday card, Gaston had thought. He spent the rest of that day in a kind of glazed reminiscence. During the week since, he had noticed that the most insignificant occurrence—a chance whiff of bacon grease, or a particular bit of phrasing in a television program—could trigger a cascade of memories, a lineage of images connecting the visible world around him to that other, lost one.

And so it happened again. As he walked, Father Gaston rubbed his hands together in the cold air, and that simple action was enough to start the memories flowing. This was the kind of day, he had once remarked to a fellow seminarian, that lent itself to the authentic contemplation of suffering, that made us more aware of it, and of its beauty and rightful place in lives lived for Christ. A day like this, therefore, was truly to be considered a privilege, he had said, a gift to be appreciated.

Gaston paused in the middle of the parking lot. So cheer up, he was thinking—hadn't that been what he meant? That suffering is a good thing? He shook his head. To be sure, he had been very young then. But did he still believe things like that? He didn't know anymore, not if he was honest with himself, and he was even a little afraid that maybe it didn't matter whether he believed such things or not. If he still thought of a priest as a man set apart, called out, he sometimes wondered what that actually meant, in this world, day to day. Maybe this questioning was a good sign.

"Father," a voice called from across the street. Gaston turned, startled and a little embarrassed to be caught mumbling to himself in the middle of an empty parking lot. A stocky man in an expensive gray overcoat approached him. The man was well groomed. He was wearing a tie. Father Gaston said nothing as he fished in his pockets for a set of rosary beads. While he waited for the man to reach him, he noticed that the rain had streaked the white walls of the rectory with gray. "Father?" the man said, putting out his hand.

Father Gaston took the man's hand gingerly. "Yes?" He had never been a vigorous shaker of hands, not like the younger priests of today, who seemed to feel they had to sell themselves like insurance men. Such openness, in Gaston's estimation, marked these priests as utterly lonely men, maybe even a little desperate. He was himself lonely, for sure. So be it. Lonely or not, he had never wanted to breach what he'd always considered an inexpressible gap between shepherd and flock.

The man appeared short of breath. "Father, do you take appointments for confession?" He spoke in quick, unnerving bursts. "Because if you do, I'd like to make one, an appointment." He looked to Gaston to be in his mid-thirties. Probably married with a couple of kids. And there was something in the man's voice—a whiff of underlying panic. Or maybe it was the voice of an uneasy sinner, someone who went around with an attitude of joviality regarding sin, someone who bragged about sexual conquests, for example, but who didn't have the courage to put away completely the suspicion that fornication or adultery was something truly serious, a mortal sin. Gaston had read somewhere that Somerset Maugham on his deathbed had called in Bertrand Russell to convince him that there was no hell, nothing to worry about.

"You're probably busy," the man said, "but I was wondering if you might have a few minutes, maybe today, if possible."

Gaston pointed vaguely over his shoulder. "Confessions are heard Saturdays, three-forty-five to four-thirty," he said, repeating what he himself had had painted in gold script on the placard in front of the chapel. He had not heard confession by special appointment for years, not unless the person lay dying and had requested last rites.

The man winced and tilted his head almost childishly.

"Can we make it tomorrow?" Gaston said.

The man looked up into the drizzle. "I don't know, Father," he said. "I'm kind of freaking out here."

Gaston sighed. "Follow me," he said and turned and walked toward the rectory. "There's a confessional inside."

The man followed. "Thanks so much, Father. I haven't been to church in a while. Actually, it's been . . . well, you could call it a very long time."

A talker, Gaston thought. Great. "What do you think of this weather?" he asked, glancing back.

The man seemed surprised by the question. "It's fine," he said. "Actually, it's not fine, is it? It's pretty lousy."

Gaston did not look back.

"Thing is, Father," the man continued, "about going church, I'm afraid the roof might fall in the first time I ever do again." He gave a hoarse chuckle, more of a grunt, really, and then began to cough loudly.

"You're Catholic?" Father Gaston asked without turning. He knew the answer.

"Oh yeah, Father. Baptized and confirmed." It was beginning to rain again. "I remember when I was a boy, before First Communion, we had to go to confession for the first time. I was confused about the penance part of it, Father. You know, I was a kid—like what?—six or so? I was saying penance every night before going to bed and in the morning. Every night five Our Fathers, ten Hail Marys, fifteen Act of Contritions. If I made a mistake, I forced myself to begin all over again. And in the morning, too. I misunderstood the priest. It was, you know, like a clerical error." The man laughed nervously. "A technical misunderstanding. After about a year of that, my mother finally found out and explained it all to me." He whistled. "What a relief."

The two of them passed independently through the gate in the low stone wall that circumscribed the rectory grounds. Some of the loose stones lay in tangles of bare honeysuckle vines. Gaston made a note to himself to repair the wall and to trim those vines back come spring.

"Now?" the man said. "I don't know. I'm a little adrift, Father."

Gaston raised his eyebrows. "Please, let's wait until we're seated in the confessional." Many times before, he had told himself that it was not his place to judge. But he knew this man's type. And more and more, this type seemed the norm— Catholics who thought of the Church as they thought of the neighborhood they had grown up in or clothes they'd lost and later found but had no intention of wearing ever again. It was all a feeling to them. Nostalgia, nothing more. Everything real to them was a feeling. If they couldn't feel something, it wasn't real. They thought of the Church as a museum, the priests as museum guides. They appreciated the beauty of the Church, but it was an inauthentic appreciation. Father Gaston knew that species of Catholic when he saw it. He fingered his rosary again and, mindful of his judging, reminded himself that it would be nice to fill the pews with a few parishioners. But he couldn't check his thoughts. These people came to confession, a rare event in itself, over something that kept them up nights. Then you'd never see them again. "The cheapest therapy in the world," one of those TV priests had said of the sacrament of confession. Gaston had never forgotten it—the smugness of that TV priest. He took a deep breath and made a note to pray later for God's help in this matter of judging. He was not the judge, just a voice.

They climbed the broad granite steps and entered the rectory. A familiar smell—of furniture polish and carpet mold—lingered in the vestibule. Gaston made a mental note to have the rugs cleaned. Another in the endless litany of chores. They followed the sound of a typewriter as it echoed along the hallway. Just as they reached the room in which the confessional stood against the wall, a telephone rang in another part of the rectory. Gaston fought the urge to walk off and answer it.

"This is the confessional that used to be in the chapel," Father Gaston explained. "We don't have one in the chapel anymore because it took up a lot of room. But now we don't need the room because no one comes to church." The man nodded silently and lowered his head. Gaston had intended the comment, not as a rebuke, but as a kind of joke, if only because it was the most he had yet said to the man. The poor guy probably regretted having picked a cranky old Canuck *prêtre* to hear his confession, Gaston thought. What luck. And then a question occurred to him: Did he even care what this man thought of him?

"These days it's fashionable to hear confession face to face," Gaston said. "The 'new way,' they say. Well, it's not all that new. And in any case, let's not do it the 'new way.'"

The man nodded, his head down.

Gaston continued, "I don't care for the face-to-face confession, unless it's absolutely necessary." For the first time he fully faced the man. "Look at me," he said, louder than he intended.

The man's head shot up, genuine fear in his eyes.

Immediately, Gaston regretted having raised his voice. "Just relax," he said, forcing a smile. He motioned to the confessional. "People would call this an antique, probably mistake it for a changing room." It looked wholly out of place among the mundane office furniture and the folding tables and chairs — like a huge, ugly armoire, though at the same time somehow strangely beautiful, the way hulking relics from the nineteenth century have become. Gaston had always thought the wood itself was the color of dried blood, and in the center of each of its dark mahogany panels had been carved a delicate rosette. Roses were the flower of the Blessed Mother. The phrase *the official flower of the Blessed Mother* ran through his head. He made a note to watch less TV.

Gaston took off his jacket, then the black cardigan sweater he wore over his black shirt. "Give me a moment before you come in. Afterward, you can leave the way we entered. Say your penance in the chapel." He smiled a little half smile. The man smiled back. "You only need to say it once." With that Gaston disappeared behind the heavy velvet curtain, which hung in deep red folds.

In the close darkness, he prepared himself both to listen and to forget, the way he'd been taught. The memories were stirring again. He thought of himself as a young priest, about the same age as the man kneeling on the other side of the thin wall. He wondered why he had never returned to the sad little seminary at St. Jean, where he had been ordained. It was always raining there. Why hadn't he kept up his correspondence with his seminary friends? Or with his teacher, for that matter? The obituary had listed not a single survivor, not a nephew or a niece — no one. Was the teacher watching him right now?

He heard the man breathing unevenly. Gaston waited for him to get settled, then tried to slide open the small door between them. It resisted at first, only to give way with a loud shudder and thud, which startled them both. But in the silence that followed, before the man began to speak, the only sound was the creak of Gaston's wooden chair as he leaned back to listen.

The man cleared his throat. "Oh, Jeez," he said. "I'm nervous. I guess it starts like this, right? Bless me, Father, for I have sinned." He paused.

"Very good," Gaston said, trying not to betray his impatience. He hadn't eaten breakfast that morning, and he realized he was hungry. "Continue."

The man fumbled. "Well."

"There's no rush," Gaston said. How unusual it seemed to him to hear English spoken in the confessional. And more than that, to hear so young a voice on the other side of the screen. For years, Gaston had been hearing, almost exclusively, the confessions of the old women, many of them nuns, at the various nursing homes in his parish, who still spoke the French of that lost world, with its nasal rhythms, its anxious tightenings and releases, its brief bursts and long quiet. "How long has it been since your last confession?" Gaston asked the man. "Simply begin at the beginning." Canadian French had a color, he was thinking, at least on the lips of those elderly nuns. It was a gray-brown hue, like that of the daguerreotypes he often saw on the old women's nightstands. It was the color of ivory crucifixes darkened by cigarette smoke.

"Father," the man began again, "I'm sorry, but I can't remember how long it's been. I couldn't tell you." Gaston felt a curious tingling spread through his shoulders and arms. At first he thought it was rage, a wash of righteous anger finally manifesting itself, but as the sensation traveled into his hands, burning and cooling his fingers, he was surprised to discover that it was nothing more than compassion for this man, who did not possess even the most basic tools. This man was lost, suffering blindly like the rest of the young people.

"More than ten years?" Gaston asked, consciously softening his tone.

The man laughed sadly. "More than twenty, Father."

"More than twenty," Gaston repeated. "That's all right." Gaston smiled in the dark, patting his own hand. "What are your sins?"

The man paused again. "The main thing is—I don't even know if it's a sin on my part, Father. I had something to do with it, but I didn't actually do it. I mean, because of me—my sin of omission, I guess it's called?—because of me this thing got done, but—"

"Slow down," Father Gaston interrupted. "What is this thing?" Sometimes, when you heard confession, Gaston reminded himself, you had to know when to listen and when to talk. And sometimes you listened by talking a little. Sometimes the slightest of words—even a sound—gave form and feeling to the gray void into which the penitent spoke. God was often too silent. Often? thought Gaston. Did He ever speak at all anymore?

"You got some time, Father?" the man asked. "This might take a little while."

"Of course," Gaston said. He nearly said, *I'm made of time,* but he caught himself. "Please, just tell me what happened."

"All right. There's this kid I hired to do repairs on a tenement house I bought last spring. I grew up in the house, Father. On the third floor of the place. I jumped when I had a chance to buy the building. This kid—kind of a punk, really—I had him clean out the attic. There was all kinds of stuff up there, what I thought was just junk from when my parents were still living there."

There was a long pause. But just as Gaston was about to prompt him, the man began again.

"I didn't have any clear idea what was up there. I'm way too busy. I sell naked furniture—that's furniture that hasn't been stained or painted, Father."

"Yes," Gaston said, "I know what naked furniture is."

"So I just told this kid Joe that he could have whatever he wanted and throw the rest out." The man caught his breath. "This is where I think the sin comes in, but I'm not sure."

"Whether or not you have actually sinned," Gaston said slowly, "please tell me what you at least *believe* to be the nature of your sin."

"I haven't slept in months, Father."

"Well, I'm sorry to hear that," Gaston said. "Please continue."

"My parents—my mother, really—she was very devoted to the Virgin Mary. It was just Virgin Mary, Virgin Mary, all the time. She collected those little statuettes of Mary, and those little laminated cards with Mary on them with the snake at her feet, wrapped around the world. From Fatima and places like that. I remember on each of our bedposts, we had all the medals hanging there. And in the stairwell, as you climbed, it must have been about twenty little statuettes on shelves she had my father build on the walls going up. And after she died, or before, maybe, I don't know, my older brother moved all this stuff up to the attic. So when Joe cleaned out the place, he found all of it—must have been a dozen boxes."

Gaston smiled. "Your mother was *Franco-Canadienne.*"

"Oh, yeah," the man said. "Big time."

Gaston sighed. "Go on."

"Well, I'll just say it," the man paused. "Later, when I asked this Joe what he did with the stuff, just out of curiosity, that's when he told me what he found up there. And then Joe tells me that he just dumped all the statues in the Acushnet River." The man cut himself off, and there was a long silence between them. "He just dumped the medals and the statuettes and everything off the Coggeshall Street bridge. He didn't keep a thing. At first I was just taken aback. But then I started thinking, and I started worrying, and that's why I'm here."

Father Gaston rested a moment as long habit dictated, pausing after the unveiling of the sin in order to bestow the pronouncement of the penance with the weight of contemplation, even though he had long ago stopped pondering the precise calculus of repentance—how many Hail Marys for unclean thoughts, how many Acts of Contrition for untruths told. He began to speak, but stopped. He could assure a penitent if need be that he as a priest had heard it all, knowing that often much of the sinner's anguish came from the belief that his actions set a new standard for sin, that he or she was the first. But something like this Gaston had not heard before. He wondered whether his hesitation arose from not knowing the source of the sin—the origin of the particular malice directed at God— or whether *that* was even a factor here. Was this a sin at all? Or would that be like calling the state of the Acushnet River, that filthy open sore of a waterway, a sin? And who could be at fault for such a thing? Who needed absolution?

"Father?" the man whispered.

Gaston was remembering again, the images falling like dead leaves. How his parents had, each year, marked the days on their calendar until their turn to host, in their home, the statue of the Blessed Virgin. How the neighbors would arrive with attitudes of profound joy, eager to kneel and to say the rosary together with his family and to stay until late into the night eating fricassee and meat pies and bread pudding. His mother's face looked at him from somewhere in the darkness of the confessional. Where has our world gone, Gaston? she seemed to ask. The question was almost an accusation. He knew the answer: It lingered in the memories of those dying sisters at Our Lady's Haven, so old and frail that they would speak only on Fridays, in barely audible whispers, requesting absolution for sins Gaston found it difficult to imagine they had the energy to commit. (He suspected they often invented sins to tell!) Far too late for such a world now, he told the face of his mother, and too much for one man to pass on. For though that lost world lived on in his memory as well, it survived in hints and fragments that made less sense with the passing of each day, like whispers from behind the deteriorating altarpiece of St. Anthony's Church, or the stillness of empty pews just before Mass on a cloudless day.

"That bad, Father?" the man said.

Gaston literally shook his head clear. "No. Let me think." His mind scrambling for words that could pass for wisdom, he settled finally for ones that might merely comfort the man on the other side of the screen. That was his job. "The images of the Blessed Virgin are not as important as the heartfelt veneration of her."

"That's what I was thinking, Father, but—"

"Without veneration," Father Gaston continued, raising his voice over the man's, and pronouncing his words slowly, carefully, "without veneration, these images are meaningless." Gaston's glowing watch dial showed that it was just after noon, and already he felt heavy and exhausted and utterly alone. He no longer heard the dry, distant snap of the typewriter. His hands lay in his lap. In the darkness they were lumpy and tender and inert, two small dying animals. "For this reason their defilement is meaningless. And besides—"

A telephone rang along the corridor.

"Really, Father?" The man's voice lightened. "Then I don't have to worry?"

"You don't have to worry," Gaston said. "Put it out of your mind." He waited for a few moments before asking the man about any other sins he might have committed in the twenty years since his last confession. But from then on, Gaston merely half listened, as he had been taught at St. Jean, and the man's voice was already fading into the muffled gnash and hiss of the father's memory, the forgotten voices and the weight of their speakable, forgotten sins.

Even as he gave the man his penance, Gaston was thinking of the statues.

The Mother of God.

A jumble of white faces. The tiny hands in the foul silt of the river bottom.

For hours the heaviness stayed with him. It was evening before Father Gaston emerged from the curtained stall of the confessional, long after he had sent the other man out into the world with a clear conscience.

BREAD LOAF AND THE BAKELESS PRIZES

The Katharine Bakeless Nason Literary Publication Prizes were established in 1995 to expand Bread Loaf Writers' Conference's commitment to the support of emerging writers. Endowed by the LZ Francis Foundation, the prizes commemorate Middlebury College patron Katharine Bakeless Nason and launch the publication career of a poet, fiction writer, and creative nonfiction writer annually. Winning manuscripts are chosen in an open national competition by a distinguished judge in each genre. Winners are published by Houghton Mifflin Company in Mariner paperback original.

2003 JUDGES

Louise Glück, poetry

Jay Parini, fiction

Ted Conover, creative nonfiction